Down the Dirt Road

Down the Dirt Road – Book 1

Authors: Livell James and Chelsea Handcock

www.chelseahandcock.com

1

Lucas Valentin has been summoned home to fulfil his duty as Guardian of the McClane Coven. He has always known that he cannot interfere with the Coven. That changes when he sees her. Drawn to her curvy beauty, he knows instantly she is his mate. The one person meant just for him but forbidden and for her own safety out of his reach.

Kaylee Smith gets one call from her Grandparents and she quits her job, packs up her things and moves to rural Alabama. She has no clue what she is walking into, never having been told the secrets of her family or that there are Others in the world. When confronted with the truth and one sexy hybrid she jumps in with two feet but he resists her.

Will Kaylee be able to get the battle-wary, sexy-as-sin, hybrid to accept her and what is meant to be? Can she have it all, her place in the Coven and the love of her life? Or will they be forced to run? Or will he run without her?

One thing is certain, life on the dirt road will never be the same.

Content Warning: Explicit love scenes, naughty language. Intended for mature audiences.

Table Of Contents

Chapter 1

Kaylee sat in her car on the side of the road, just off her exit in nowhere Alabama, staring at the sign in front of her—Eclectic twenty miles. The old wood sign had seen better days; it had bullet holes decorating it, and the paint was chipped and peeling in places. She couldn't believe she was here. She couldn't believe she had left behind the only life she had ever known.

This was the right thing to do. That was what Kaylee Smith needed to keep reminding herself of over and over again. Or at least until the words took root and stuck, but there was a part of her which knew they never would. It might be the right thing and something she didn't have a problem doing, per se, but leaving her life behind was wearing on her like the miles she travelled down this dirt road. This trip wasn't a simple visit; she was moving her life here, to Eclectic, Alabama. Home of basically nothing, but her grandparents and trees.

Two weeks ago, she had been working her job at the bank as a teller, a typical nine-to-five job. It wasn't much, but it paid the bills and gave her a sense of independence. The apartment she lived in was nothing special either, but it was hers, filled with the things she loved. Now, most of those things were crammed into her tiny Ford Escape while the rest had been donated or thrown out.

Her Grandma had called and told Kaylee they needed her, and without a second thought, she jumped into action to make that happen. Her grandparents were getting up there in age, and their health wasn't the best. Kaylee was most concerned about her grandpa. According to her grandma, he hadn't been doing very well lately and that greatly concerned her.

Kaylee's mom, their only daughter, lived in California and had a killer job, so the responsibility of caring for them fell to Kaylee. At least that's what she kept telling herself and everyone else; the truth was her mom was selfish and couldn't be bothered to help out her own parents. No, that responsibility was always laid on Kaylee's shoulders. Not that she minded, she loved her grandparents and would do anything for them. Even leave behind all her friends and the fantastic nightlife and restaurants of Birmingham. It was a small price to pay for the people who you love and cherish, right?

That was the other reason she was sitting on the side of the road; she had a call to make. Hitting the redial button on her steering wheel, Kaylee tried to keep positive thoughts in her mind. This time her mother would answer her call; she had only been trying to get ahold of the woman for two weeks. On the fourth ring, she slammed her hand down on the button, disconnecting the call. She refused to leave another message which would go unanswered.

She and her mother had a very contentious relationship. The woman was never there when Kaylee needed her that responsibility was always left to her Grandma Ruth. Another reason why she left her life behind and came to Eclectic, of all places; she owed her even though Kaylee knew her grandmother wouldn't say or feel that way, Kaylee did, so that was that.

Kaylee hated driving long distances, but thankfully most of the drive was behind her now. She knew the rest of the ride would be leisurely. Only long, scenic backroads were ahead with beautiful cotton fields and pastures filled with horses and cows. She could take her time and enjoy the scenery as long as she got to her grandparents sometime today or they would worry. She had her mega sized Diet Coke and she was going to take her time. Plan set, she put her car in drive and pulled back out onto the road; only little longer now she thought. Looking at all the familiar landmarks, she let her mind wander to happier times.

As a child, she visited her grandparents often. Every time she got in trouble or her mother needed a break, she shipped her off to her Grandma Ruth. Kaylee often wondered why the woman had decided to have a child in the first place. Her time spent with her Grandparents, those were memories she cherished.   Kaylee could remember getting so excited once they hit the dirt road leading to her grandparents' home. The feeling was still there, and the closer she got, the excitement bubbling up in her stomach was giving her butterflies.

She was so caught up in her memories of the past, her phone ring loudly in the silent car scared the crap out of her. She jumped, spilling her drink all over the front of her, the cool liquid pooling in her cleavage and seat.

"Son of a pup!" Kaylee yelled. She thought it might be her mother calling her back, so she hit the button on her steering wheel to engage her phone, but ended up hitting the wrong button, disconnecting the call. "Damn it," Kaylee barked to herself. If it was her mother, she could wait for once.

Kaylee squirmed in her soaked pants and shirt. Looking over in the passenger seat, she tried to find something to wipe herself, but didn't see anything. Glancing in the back, she saw a sweatshirt she had thrown back there which seemed within reach. Doing some contortionist moves, trying to reach back and still keep her eyes on the road, she managed to get her hands on the garment. But like with all good plans, something went wrong. She must have looked away for just a second because the next thing she knew, she was slamming on the brakes.

"Oh Fuck!", Kaylee screamed. There was a man standing right in the middle of the road. Well, he had been just a second ago, now, he was laying on the side of the road somewhere. Kaylee jump out of the car, barely putting it in park first, running to the other side of the car. She knew she hadn't hit him, but he was still on the ground. What was he doing out here in the middle of nowhere, standing in the middle of the road?

"Oh my God, I am so sorry, are you okay?" She offered the prone man her hand, only to pull it back when that small touch produced a massive static shock. She could have sworn she even heard the snap, she sure felt it. Rubbing her hand on her wet jeans, she tried again; this time when he took her hand, it only tingled.

When he finally stood to his full height, Kaylee was pretty sure her mouth was hanging wide open. This man didn't belong in the middle of rural Alabama. He belonged on a stage somewhere, guitar firmly in hand, stroking and strumming it, while he held it close. That brought a few other thoughts to her mind. Shaking her head, Kaylee couldn't believe she was so all over the place. She had just scared the crap out of both of them, now she was drooling over him, like a groupie.

"Are you okay?" she asked for the second time,

The guy was looking at her with a small grin on his face, but he didn't say anything, making her more concerned. She must have done something or made a noise because he finally spoke.

"I'm fine ma'am, just a little shaken up, no harm done," he said releasing her hand and brushing off his extremely tight jeans. Damn, where was her head, she wasn't acting like herself at all. She didn't notice how tight strange men's jeans were. She wasn't that type of girl.

Sure, she paid attention when a good-looking guy crossed her path, but this was different, this man was different. He was a work of art—from his shiny, long black hair, flipped to the side, framing his face to the brightly colored tattoos decorating his arms, peeking out of his unbuttoned shirt. Argh, she almost wanted to slap herself.

Kaylee couldn't have stopped looking if she wanted to, the man compelled her eyes to stay on him. It was as if he put a spell on her, it was weird but also comforting, like she had found something she had been looking for all her life. As he walked closer to her, everything else seemed to fade away until they were the only two people in the world. His eyes were a color of blue she had only seen when she visited the ocean and could only be described as piercing, drawing her in further. Kaylee felt a feather light touch on her cheek, drawing her back to reality.

"Are you okay?" the man asked. Oh, my Lord, his voice was amazing. Deep and raspy, it sent shivers down her spine. Kaylee just stared for a second, unable to speak or move. When he laughed, she shook her head.

"Yeah, I guess this whole thing freaked me out more than I thought," Kaylee said waving her hand toward the car and then back at the man. "Sorry, but what were you doing in the middle of the road? I wasn't going that fast, and I only looked away for a second. I know I didn't hit you, but then you were on the other side of the road laying down. You scared the shit out of me."

Kaylee knew she was rambling. She thought about the words she was saying and what was going on here. She was in the middle of nowhere with a man who stood in front of an oncoming car, only to throw himself off to the side. It was like the start of a bad slasher film.

Stepping away, she started going back to her car and safety. She knew better than this, she should have at least gotten her phone or called 911 before she got out of the car. Didn't con men do this stuff all the time to get a little free cash? She started walking a little faster now her brain had finally engaged.

It didn't matter that the man was gorgeous and was wearing tight as sin, skinny jeans. Or that those jeans hugged his calves and thighs, showing everything while still leaving some mystery of what she would find underneath. She needed to get the hell out of here, but a part of her wanted to stay right there with this man.

The man kept following her, picking up speed as she did. Well, he didn't really need to pick up speed. His legs were so long, she was pretty sure three of her steps equaled one of his. Just as she made it to the door of her car, he grabbed her elbow to stop her, but let go quickly.

"Listen, I'm sorry, I had some shit on my mind and wasn't really paying attention. Not many people come down this road. I live right over there," he pointed and Kaylee squinted, trying to see what he was pointing at.

Kaylee could barely make out a house; well, she wasn't actually seeing it now. The woods engulfed it, she was only getting a peek of the hunter green, metal roofline sticking out above the treetops. It looked like it had been there forever, but she had been down this dirt road so many times before, yet she had never once noticed it.

"My name is Lucas, sorry for scaring you."

Kaylee put one hand on the handle to open her car door, waving the other one. "No problem Lucas, I apologize, too, but I really need to get going, unless you would like me to call 911 or something?" Kaylee needed to ask. Lucas didn't look any worse for wear, but...

"No, I'm fine," he said as he started walking away toward the house he'd pointed out.

Thinking or not really thinking because this whole experience was extremely odd, Kaylee yelled out her name. When he turned around, but kept walking backward, he raised his eyebrow, asking her a question. "My name, it's Kaylee. It was nice to meet you, Lucas, wish it had been under better circumstances."

"See you around Kaylee Smith, I've heard a lot about you, can't wait to learn a lot more" Lucas smiled, then took off running. Why had he heard about her? Kaylee just stood there for a second, not really knowing what to think. This was a small town and her Grandma loved to gossip; he lived close, maybe that was how he knew her name or anything about her. How freaking odd?

Getting back in the car, she put it in drive, only this time driving well below the speed limit. She felt weird. Kaylee was even more excited now about her decision to come here. There was a warmth which radiated through her body as if this visit would change her life in some way. An intuition she couldn't put her finger on, but she could feel something big was about to happen. Maybe it had something to do with the man she just left?

Seeing the last turnoff to her grandparent's home, she smiled; Kaylee was finally here. Pushing her foot down on the accelerator, Kaylee continued down the dirt road.

Kaylee pulled into the long driveway, and once the house came into view, she stopped to take it all in. The house had been in her family for generations. Her great grandpa had built it by hand over a hundred years ago, using the trees in the area to make logs which eventually created the exterior. It had been a labor of love, completely built by hand with little help; she admired the outcome. Her grandparents had updated it through the years, but the rustic charm was still there.

Seeing her grandma on the porch, waving at her, brought a smile to her face so full, it hurt her cheeks. Kaylee waved back and heard her grandma yelling, "Edwin get up here, Kaylee is here!" Putting her car in park, Kaylee jumped out of the car, running to greet Ruth.

Her Grandma Ruth never changed, still wearing her token apron, her gray hair twisted up in a bun. Kaylee knew once she got close enough, the sweet rose smell of her perfume would engulf her nose. What Kaylee really needed was to hear that sweet, southern twang in her grandmas' voice when she uttered Kaylee's name. When Kaylee was close enough, she launched herself at Ruth, hugging her for all she was worth. Her grandma pulled back, holding Kaylee at arm's length.

"Oh, child, what happened to you?

Kaylee had been so excited, she had totally forgotten the sticky mess coating her clothes and body. Kaylee waved her hand, brushing it off and said, "It's nothing, just spilled my drink. Where's Grandpa? I can't wait to see him," Kaylee said excitedly.

"Oh, Kaylee, he gets tired more quickly now. He and Lucas have been working on your cabin ever since you told me you were coming. He'll be back up in a bit. It takes him awhile to get moving."

9

Kaylee was disappointed. She wanted to see her grandpa, but she understood; this was the reason she was here. She didn't like that he was working so hard, wearing himself out for something meant for her, but that would change now. Then she recalled what else her grandma had said.

"Lucas?" Kaylee questioned. She was pretty sure that Lucas was not a common name around these parts. She was also pretty sure she had already met the Lucas her Grandma was talking about.

"Oh, hon, we had to hire someone to help us do all the work around here. Lucas has been a godsend. He lives right down the road and comes over every day to see if we need anything."

"I think I might have just met him up the road a bit when I almost ran him over with my car," Kaylee laughed

"What?" Grandma Ruth gasped.

"Yep, he was standing in the middle of the road, and I had to slam on my brakes to avoid hitting him."

"Oh, Kaylee, you really need to be more careful." Kaylee chuckled at that. Her Grandma Ruth was a menace behind the wheel; Kaylee not so much.

"I know, Grandma," Kaylee said, hugging her again. When they started walking towards the house, arm and arm, Kaylee asked, "So this Lucas, what's he like?"

"Oh, he's a nice boy, I guess, hard worker and all."

The short answer bewildered Kaylee; her Grandma was a gossip, but she wasn't saying much about Lucas. Maybe she needed to look into the guy a little after all. Maybe her thoughts about him being a con man weren't all that far off base, but he didn't give her that weird creepy vibe. He gave her another vibe all together, one she wasn't really sure she wanted to think about with her grandma so close.

"I saw his house or part of it. It's pretty far back in the woods. Funny, I never noticed it before."

"Oh, Kaylee, you haven't been here in so long, things have changed. The Valentin's have had that house for several decades."

Huh, Kaylee thought, still seemed weird to her that she had never noticed it before. She was a watcher, always had been. People, places, things—it didn't matter, she watched. She could pick out trees along the road which were familiar just by their shapes, but that house, not even a small memory. It didn't make any sense.

Chapter 2

Lucas had been working with Edwin when he got the strangest urge to go to the road. His beast was calling to him, and it wouldn't be denied. He made his excuses and took off. When he found himself standing in the middle of the road with an SUV coming straight at him, he was dumbfounded for a second. His body tightened, and he couldn't move. Lucas didn't sense a threat, but he did sense something, he just couldn't put his finger on it. Drawing his brows together, he tried to see through the windshield, but the sun's glare was making it impossible. All his senses were pinging on the car or rather the occupant of the car, and he willed himself to see better, clearer, trying to make the impossible possible. What the hell was going on?

His first instinct was to charge forward, stopping the car with his bare hands, but he held himself back. He had never reacted this way in his life and couldn't figure out what was going on now, but just as the car came closer, he realized, at the last second, whoever it was, wasn't going to stop. Stepping off to the side of the road, his foot caught on something, and he fell. Seconds later, he heard the screech of tires, making him cringe.

When the door of the Escort burst open and a blur of blonde hair and curves darted toward him, Lucas was floored. His jaw dropped, his hands clenching at his sides in tight fists as though he was trying to hold his body back from getting up and running straight for her. His thigh muscles bunched and contracted with the effort to stay in one place.

The woman was beautiful, so beautiful in fact, Lucas hadn't realized he'd stopped breathing until his amulet started to burn the shit out of his chest, causing him to come back to the here and now. She was saying something to him, but he didn't hear the words. He could only look at her, taking everything in. What the hell! Lucas loved women of all shapes and sizes, but he had never had this kind of response to one, not even close.

Wrapping his hand around his amulet, he allowed the burn to sink into his hand. She was kind of short for his tastes. Lucas had always liked tall women, he was never attracted to short, tiny ones like this lady. He would have to turn himself into a pretzel just to kiss her, but he knew it would be worth the effort. None of his previous feelings or tastes made a damn bit of difference now. This chick was just right as far as he was concerned. He felt his canines drop from his gums, pricking his lip. The sting caused him to grunt in pain, but made him focus. He needed to get his shit together because she was coming right at him, full speed. Showing a human his Otherness was not permitted, for any reason.

He had a duty to the McClanes and his pack to keep his secrets well-hidden, or he would be facing more than just a slap on the wrist. Allowing humans, other than mates, to know about his abilities or other forms was against Pack law and punishable by death. Something his Alpha would gladly carry out. Breathing slowly, he concentrated on his thoughts and not his senses because right now all those senses were pinging on the tiny blonde.

His beast was clawing at him to move, to get closer, and scent the air. When the urge was too great, he couldn't have stopped himself if he tried. Lucas lifted his nose into the air, needing to imprint her unique scent into his soul. The sweet smell of honeysuckle invaded him, wrapping him in a calm he had never felt before; his mouth watered for a taste. Shaking his head, he chastised himself for thinking this way. She wasn't fried chicken, after all, she was just a woman. An extraordinary woman, but a woman just the same.

Groaning, he felt all the blood in his body pooling in his groin, making the calm he felt for a fraction of a second evaporate just as quickly. He wasn't a teenager, he was fucking twenty-seven. He had been controlling his body for years. It was embarrassing.

When she offered him her hand, there wasn't a force on earth which would have stopped him from taking it. The shock which coursed through his body the moment their hands met was breathtaking. He wasn't a poetic guy, but it was as if Zeus himself had shot a lightning bolt right through the two of them, binding them together. When she pulled away, he almost growled.

That was enough to stop him in his tracks. He needed to block her out, get his shit together, and get the hell out of here. But he also needed her touch. When she offered her hand a second time, he held on a little tighter. He didn't need any help getting up, he just wanted to feel her touch.

When her mouth fell open a little as she took him in, Lucas smiled. Maybe he wasn't the only one affected. He could smell her honeysuckle scent deepen, become headier with her arousal.

Lucas stood and adjusted himself covertly, not wanting the woman to think he was a pervert or something worse. She might be attracted to him, but she was also human. Weres and Vamps were different; as long as the attraction was there and both parties were in agreement, neither would hesitate to take this attraction further. But this woman wasn't putting off any vibes she was looking for a hook up of any kind. Her reaction to him though, hell, that made him feel ten-feet tall.

Lucas decided to focus on her face, it seemed the safest thing to do. Were and Vampire, he had excellent vision, hearing, and strength, but distance caused distortion. That's why he hadn't been able to see her through the windshield of her car, well, that and the sun. Now, he realized there was something to be said about an up close and personal view.

He could see the light green specks in her expressive, but hooded blue eyes framed by black glasses, along with the small spattering of freckles decorating her tiny nose. Her perfectly glossed lips were supple and plump. Right now, the bottom one was more pronounced as she pursed them together. Her little pink tongue was peeking out of the corner as if she was concentrating extremely hard. Fuck, the sight made him think of other things those lips and tongue could do to him and put him right back where he started; maybe he needed to just not look at her at all.

But damn, her blatant perusal of his body made him smile wider, and his dick, the bastard, became even harder. A few seconds ago, he would have doubted that was even possible. He was wrong. When she focused on that part of him, he couldn't help the little growl of approval which escaped his throat. He and his beast liked what she was doing, and he figured what the hell, two could play this game. Lucas let his eyes wander over the woman, the curves he noticed before generous. Fuck, they were more than generous.

When her eyes met his for the first time, he couldn't help smiling at her, letting her know that, yeah, he knew exactly what she'd been doing. He was grateful she hadn't looked up sooner and caught him doing the same. But then everything quickly changed. He could smell the fear coming off of her in waves and knew he needed to do something. When she started to walk away, he couldn't let her go, so he followed and offered an apology and introduction. He really wanted to know who this woman was. When she didn't offer her name, he decided it was probably better to walk away. She might entice him like no other, but he wasn't a creeper.

Before he got too far away, she called out to him, making his day. He couldn't remember the last time he had smiled so much. There wasn't much in his life to smile about, but almost getting hit by this woman and meeting her for the first time made him happy.

Now that he knew her name, he also knew exactly who she was. Ruth and Edwin had been talking about her nonstop for the last couple of weeks as he worked by Edwin's side fixing up the old cabin. He knew they loved her dearly, but that she was also only coming out of a misguided belief Edwin was ill. Lucas didn't like deception on any scale, it had been the story of his life for way too long. He preferred honesty in all things. He didn't blame the old couple, but he still didn't like it. No one should be blindsided the way Kaylee was about to be.

Lucas Valentin had grown up knowing exactly what he was and what was expected of him. He was a Were, a man who changed into a beast, more specifically a wolf. But most importantly, he was the Guardian of the witches, the highest honor among his kind. Chosen at birth, Lucas was given the amulet currently resting on his chest right above his heart. He didn't know much about the object except it held untold power and allowed him to walk in the daylight; he wasn't just a Were, he was also a Vampire.

It was unheard of and he was loathed because he hadn't been strong enough to resist "him." Lucas felt the shiver run up his spine just thinking about "him" and what had happened that fateful day. He hated those memories and hated what he had become. Concentrating on where he was going, he took off at a greater speed, knowing Kaylee wouldn't see him now. Lucas tried to shake himself out of the past. He needed to concentrate on his job because it looked like his newest charge had just gotten to town. He would do just that, protect the McClane's at all costs. He hadn't made it very far before Edwin came into view.

"Guardian, you know better than this. She's off limits to your kind," Edwin McClane said. He wasn't a powerful Warlock, but he was a part of the McClane Coven, and Lucas had a duty to him, so he stopped and addressed the man.

"I know my place, Edwin, I also know Kaylee is different, special."

"Oh, and how do you know that, Lucas?" Edwin said with a sneer.

"I don't know, Edwin," pulling his shirt aside he revealed his amulet, "maybe you can explain to me why my amulet just changed from smoky quartz to amethyst and burned the hell out of my chest when she arrived, and I got her scent. Then maybe we can talk about how off limits your granddaughter is to me."

Lucas didn't give Edwin a chance to reply, instead he stormed off. By the time he made it to the forest edge, he didn't have any choice but to shift. His animal and vampire were playing havoc with him and needed to be set free. Stripping himself of his clothes, he shifted. Looking back in animal form, he could see a figure at the window of Kaylee's room, and he howled out his pain at being denied. Lucas ran as fast as his four legs would take him away from Kaylee.

Chapter 3

Kaylee was exhausted, confused, and sticky. She really needed to jump in the shower and change her clothes, but her mind kept drifting back to the man on the dirt road, Lucas. Kaylee couldn't wrap her head around why the man wouldn't leave her thoughts. He was a stranger, a gorgeous one, but still a stranger.

Being back her in her grandparents' home and why she was here should be the only thing taking up her brain space right now. Stripping off her clothes, Kaylee cringed. Going to the tiny attached bathroom, she took a quick shower. She had no sooner gotten dressed in some warm comfy clothes when she heard a knock at the bedroom door. Kaylee turned just as Grandma walked through, holding a cup in her hand.

Kaylee smiled; she had missed her grandma and being here in this house, and without Lucas as a distraction, was brought back to why she was here in the first place. Walking over to the bed, Kaylee sat down, and Grandma followed her, putting her arm around her, hugging her tightly.

"Here, little one, I brought this up for you."

Kaylee smelled the mint and knew this was her grandma's special blend of tea. When she stayed here as a child, Grandma always made it for her; it was a cherished memory.

"Thank you, but you didn't have to do this for me. I was going to get cleaned up, then come down and help you with dinner.

"Oh, hon," Grandma patted her thigh and smiled, "it's been a long, hard day for you with all that driving and your little scare on the road. I thought you would like a little tea and maybe a nap before we even thought about making any fuss for dinner. Grandpa is still out, so we still have some time."

Kaylee thought about that for a minute; why hadn't her grandpa been here to greet her? She could have sworn Grandma had called to him when she arrived, but she hadn't seen hide nor hair of the man.

"What's up with the old coot why haven't I seen him yet?" Kaylee tried to make light, but her feelings were hurt.

"Oh, hon, you know him, he's always tinkering around, doing something or other. He'll show up, you just have to give it time. He and

Lucas have been working on the cabin for weeks, getting it just right for you. He wouldn't want to disappoint his favorite granddaughter, you know."

"I'm his only granddaughter, Grandma." Her grandma looked at her funny, but Kaylee didn't want to talk about it anymore and said under her breath, "I just kind of wanted to see him, you know."

Kaylee felt the burn of tears behind her eyes. Maybe she was more tired than she thought. Grandpa was always wandering about. This wasn't the first time he hadn't been there when Kaylee arrived, and she was pretty sure it wouldn't be the last, but she still couldn't help feeling a little sorry for herself. She had come here because he was ill; she wanted to get a good look at him for herself.

She and Grandma chatted for a while, and Kaylee was getting really tired by the time she finished her tea, she was practically asleep sitting up. She felt Grandma help her lay down and was helpless to do anything, but drift off to a pleasant sleep. She heard her grandma close the door and the sound of her feet going down the stairs.

Kaylee was so warm and comfortable, she didn't want to move. As her body relaxed into the bed, she couldn't help but moan in satisfaction as she snuggled further down in the blankets. This was like lying on a beach with the sun soaking into her body and the best massage rolled into one, and yet, she was only lying there in bed, falling asleep. Her mind flickered to a strange thought, what was different about this time?

Moving her legs, she rubbed them against the silk covered bed, marveling at the feel against her legs. The silky caress amplified the amazing feeling. There was a small part of her brain which couldn't place the silky bedding, but the feeling overwhelmed her, and the thought soon fled, leaving her in a blissful state.

She moaned in delight, everything felt so right against her body. Even the sturdy, toasty wall at her back brought her comfort and joy. Hey, wait just a minute, sturdy, toasty wall? Kaylee struggled against it until she heard a whisper in her ear.

"Wake up, Kaylee, it's time."

Time? Time for what she wondered, but she knew that voice or at least thought she did. Lucas? Kaylee tried to get up and move away from the man. She might recognize his voice, but he was still a stranger.

Nothing she did seemed to move her body away from him. Getting a little scared, she asked, "Lucas, how, are you here, why are you here?"

"Shh, sweet girl, let me take care of you."

Those words and the sound of his deep, growly timbre, made her fears melt away. It also caused a reaction in her body she wasn't ready for. Her breast became heavy and her nipples beaded into painful, diamond points. Kaylee moaned, rubbing her thighs together, desperate to relieve the ache. She felt his long, adept fingers slowly rub up the inside of her thighs, pulling them slightly apart. She knew on some level, she should stop this, stop him, but the warmth of his body and the natural scent of him—woodsy with just a hint of musk—enticed her. The movement of his fingers as he ran them up higher on her thigh intrigued her and, she realized she didn't want him to stop. Kaylee felt his warm breath on the shell of her ear before she heard his whispered words.

"I want you, all of you."

Kaylee whimpered at his declaration, parting her legs a little further, encouraging him to move them to where she needed them most. Then he stopped, and Kaylee cried out in frustration.

The warm wet kiss to her shoulder caused another sensation, distracting her from the disappointment she felt. Arching her hips further, giving him more room to explore, Kaylee groaned when feather soft lips move to her ear and nip, causing shocks of pleasure to erupt all over her body.

"Let me take you. Let me feel you," Lucas said as he continued to nibble on her ear and worked his way back down her neck, moving his hand to the place where she could lose herself in the ecstasy Kaylee knew his talented fingers would provide. But his touch was still so light and not nearly what she needed. When she started to squirm again, Lucas moved his hand back down her thigh and squeezed it firmly.

"Shh, Kaylee, settle, let me do this for you. Concentrate on how good I can make you feel when you just let go."

Kaylee nodded, words completely useless to her, she was so caught up in the moment. She realized she wanted this, she wanted Lucas to touch her and give her everything he promised. Kaylee did as he asked and let go. Let her body go slack for whatever he planned next.

As a reward, Lucas kissed her neck and pulled her closer into his heat. Kaylee could feel the heavy weight of his molten staff as he ground against her ass. The slight dampness leaking from the tip showed his need and want for her.

Kaylee could feel her own arousal increase, wetting her thighs. Lucas was in full control now, and she was surprised how natural it all felt. His words and whispers became more of a growl as she felt him move away a little, only to pull her onto her back. Kaylee cupped his cheek, looking directly into his eyes.

The noises he was making should have scared her—it wasn't natural, he was growling like an animal—but they didn't. They made her feel safe and cherished. His blue eyes brightened and changed to a burnished gold and like the first time, drew her deeper into him. His rough, calloused hand cupped her breast as if testing its heavy weight.

"So beautiful, Kaylee."

Kaylee bowed her back, pushing her breast into his hand, begging him with her actions to continue. Lucas smiled down at her, but shook his head.

"Shh, Kaylee."

Bringing his body over hers, she relished the weight of his taut, muscular frame on her own. His touch was still soft, but commanding. As he settled in the apex of her thighs, Kaylee let her hands roam, feeling every part of him she could reach. His moan only encouraged her to continue with the delightful journey.

The moment their bodies met was pure bliss. The world outside didn't matter anymore, the only thing which mattered was them together, and Lucas taking her, claiming her for the first time.

"Do you want this, Kaylee, do you want me to claim you as mine?"

Kaylee smiled, he knew she did, but he was going to make her say it, beg. It seemed to be his way, and she didn't have a problem asking for what she needed.

"Please, Lucas, make me yours, give everything to me, I want it all of it. I want to be yours, I want to feel you inside of me. Please, Lucas."

Bringing her legs up, she circled his waist and ground herself against his hard shaft. Lucas groaned, leaning down, kissing her lips. A chaste kiss, at first, but Kaylee wanted, needed more. Opening her mouth, she brought her tongue out to play with his fuller bottom lip, nipping him with her teeth when he didn't take the hint to take the kiss further. Kaylee could feel Lucas' smile against her mouth.

"I see slow and sweet isn't what you're looking for." Kaylee never got a chance to reply as he devoured her mouth, taking the once sweet kiss to a level which took Kaylee's breath away. There wasn't a part of her mouth he didn't explore with his tongue, teeth, and lips, and Kaylee was so lost to the sensations, she didn't care she needed air to breathe, she just wanted this kiss to continue forever. When he ended the kiss and smiled at her, she was lost, once again. This man was gorgeous, every tattooed inch of him.

"Are you ready to fly, my sweet girl?" Lucas whispered.

Kaylee pretty much thought she was already flying, but nodded. She could feel him at her entrance and with just one short thrust, fireworks exploded behind her eyes. His head was buried in her neck, and he was breathing heavily.

Lucas took her hands in his, pulling them above her head and laced his fingers with hers, pushing them into the bed with force, while he continued to thrust into her body. Kaylee lit up like a roman candle. He was so deep inside her, she was sure he was kissing her womb.

When he started to lose his rhythm and his movements became frantic, Kaylee watched as he bent his head back and howled. The sound, along with the blast of heat she felt in her womb, threw her over the edge, again, causing Kaylee to black out, a contented sigh on her lips.

"KAYLEE!! HEY!!! KAYLEE!!"

Pounding and a voice from outside the room made the bliss Kaylee had been feeling disappear. The warmth she had been feeling dissipated, leaving Kaylee cold and confused. She wanted to shut her eyes and go back to wherever she'd been. Her mind still heavy with sleep, Kaylee said his name, just once, but it seemed important.

"Kaylee, are you awake? It's time for dinner." Grandma Ruth voice kept getting louder, the pounding on the door more insistent.

Kaylee looked around the room and down at her still-dressed body. Bringing her hand up, she pushed the sweaty mess of hair away from her face, still trying to wrap her head around what had just happened.

"Why are you yelling for Lucas?" Grandma yelled through her door.

It couldn't have been only a dream, could it? Kaylee could still feel his touch, his kiss, but it was, it had all been just a dream. Her body quaked and shivered as she came crashing back to reality. Why in the hell was she having a sex dream about a virtual stranger? Not only a sex dream, but the best sex dream of her life. She was mortified because her Grandma was standing right outside the door. Hell, she'd lived on her own for years and never once had this happened, well, at least not to this extent. Why now, why him?

Kaylee knew she needed to acknowledge her Grandma or the woman would be barge in at any second.

"Sorry, Grandma, just a dream. I think that little scare on the road got to me a little more than I thought. Give me a second, and I'll be right down." Yeah, that sounded plausible, she just hoped her grandma bought it. Holding her breath, she waited until she heard the creak on the steps and knew Grandma Ruth was walking away. Thank you for small favors.

Chapter 4

Lucas ran hard, trying to restrain and calm his beast. The bastard wanted to go back and claim what was his, Kaylee, but Lucas wasn't ready; hell, he didn't know if he would ever be ready. Shifting back to his human form, he huffed his annoyance at his naked state. It was a common occurrence in the shifter world, a fact of life for them, all of them. His state of undress left him with another problem, his Alpha and Father. Lucas had been forbidden to shift on his own.

He was hesitant; Lucas didn't want any of the pack to catch even the slightest hint of Kaylee's scent. He wanted to keep her to himself for just a little while longer. The Pack would need to know she'd arrived, but not yet. Feeling drained from his wayward emotions, Lucas chose not to shift back into his beast form and started running through the woods. Probably not the smartest thing to do with his junk flopping from side to side and his fangs still pressing against his lips. But hell, he couldn't find the will to give a shit at the moment.

He needed to come up with a plan for when he got back to his pack's home. He didn't think of it as his home, not anymore, but the pack's house. He wasn't accepted, only tolerated because of his Guardian status. A status only the witches could remove from him, much to his father's displeasure.

Every day, the man insisted on belittling or taunting Lucas, trying to get him to do something stupid, like challenging him. That day would come, his father just didn't know it yet. His father wanted everyone to believe Lucas' vampire side made him weak or less than a full-blooded shifter, but the truth was it made him stronger. From the very beginning, the moment he had been changed, Lucas knew he needed to keep that to himself.

His biggest obstacle was the pack itself. He needed their backing to remove his father, and right now, he didn't have it. Marcus made sure of that by isolating him and spinning tales regarding Lucas' weakness. His brother, Matthias, didn't help, going along with dear old Dad, spinning just as many horrid little stories.

The pack consisted of seven males and two females, each having a very defined role. Lucas' father, Marcus, was the Alpha and ruler of their pack. His dictates were to be followed, or he dished out extreme punishments. He wasn't a good man, just the opposite. Lucas hated him. Matthias was the prince of the pack; he and Lucas might be twins, but Matthias was the favored son. Matt was Marcus' only wanted child. Matt was so intent on gaining and keeping Marcus' favor, it made it hard for Lucas to remember he loved his twin brother.

If it were not for Kaylee's Ostara ceremony, Lucas would have stayed away. The timing couldn't have been any worse, but his duty to the witches prevented him from doing so. As it was, he had only been back in Eclectic for three months, and already, his father's stifling reign had him feeling collared and cornered, not a good feeling for a man who was an animal at heart.

The Valentin pack itself wasn't as bad as their leader. Eric, the Beta, was a good person, but he could only do so much. Marcus didn't like anyone questioning how he did things. If someone was brave enough to, his response was to cause pain.

Emily was Marcus' bitch in every sense of the word. Early on, Lucas had noticed she tried to divert Marcus's attention away from him by enticing Marcus in other ways, but lately, she had stopped trying.

Danica, the only other female, was submissive to her core. She was also the healer and caretaker of the pack. Danica had an inner strength and sweetness which astounded Lucas.

Then there were the enforcers, Dylan and Macon, both good men. They had been Lucas' best friends growing up, but once he was bitten, they turned their backs on him, just like the others. Since coming back, there had been a couple of times the playful banter between them reared up, but they were few and far between; Marcus made sure of that.

Flynn was the last of the group; he was the Omega. His powers of empathy and compassion were meant to calm and bring the pack together, but even he wasn't that good. Marcus treated the man worse than he did Lucas and that was saying something.

Lucas stopped running, his mind a little clearer, and decided he needed to go back for his clothes. Maybe he could get one more glimpse at Kaylee before he had to face the pack and his isolation for the night. Taking a couple of deep breaths, Lucas noticed his heart rate had slowed, and his panting from the long hard run had stopped. He started to walk at a much slower pace, letting the breeze cool his heated flesh.

There was a trail between the pack house and the cabin he and Edwin had been working on for Kaylee and the small road at the edge of the woods which led back up to the McClane's house. Stopping for a moment, he decided taking the trail was the best way. The road wasn't often traveled, but finding a six-foot-four naked man running around would surely bring attention Lucas didn't need right now.

The trees were thick and lined both sides of the trail, making it the right choice for his streaking. He hadn't walked long when he came to a clearing. This place was sacred to both the witches and the pack. On the night of the Ostara ceremony, he knew Ruth would wave her hand and an emblazoned pentagram would appear beneath the grass. Lucas didn't need to wait for that to happen, he saw the sacred place clear as day, a benefit of his guardianship. Only he and the McClane witches had this ability, to everyone else, it was just barren land.

On the nights of the full moon, his pack, minus him, would also gather in this place to renew and rejoice. The full moon didn't make a Were shift, it was more of a beacon they needed to celebrate. Just another way Lucas was kept on the outside. He couldn't go out at night because the urge to feed was too immense for his vampire side. At least, that's what his father told everyone. At one time, it had been true, but Lucas had battled that need and impulse and won. He now had control of both his sides.

Lucas continued to walk until he was back at the beginning where he had met up with Edwin. Looking at the ground, he found his shirt; it had been ripped to shreds, there was no way he could wear it now. His pants, on the other hand, only showed a few small tears and would at least cover his exposed junk for his trek back. He didn't even bother looking for underwear because he hated them and hardly ever wore any. Being a shifter, it was imperative they could shift swiftly, and underwear just got in the way.

Dressing, he turned around to head for the pack house, but kept moving forward instead, until he found himself by the shed on the McClanes property. Looking at the house, he let his mind drift and his set his senses free. He just wanted one more peek at the woman who had changed his life so abruptly. He could smell her honeysuckle scent on the wind and took it in, much like he had before. Looking up at the windows of the house, he instantly honed in on her room.

He just wanted to get a little look before he went back to the cold hell he knew awaited him back at the pack house, but much to his disappointment, no movement or light was coming from the window. Just as he was turning away, he heard it, her voice yelling his name.

He wanted to charge into the house, take her, claim her, but held himself back. Seconds later, he heard Ruth's curt voice asking why Kaylee had been calling out his name. Knowing Edwin would be watching, Lucas' quickly made his way back to the trail and forced himself to keep moving away from Kaylee; now wasn't the time.

Walking at a faster pace, Lucas took a shortcut through the woods. The sun was going down, and he knew he needed to get inside soon. Once his foot breached Valentin land, he knew what he would find, his father waiting for him all six-foot tall, muscle-bound part of him.

To some, Marcus Valentin might be considered a nice-looking man, to Lucas he was anything but. What he saw was the hate and greed which marred his father's eyes. His once black hair was now salt-and-pepper, his smooth face covered with craggy wrinkles. His body looked unnatural for a man of his age, beefed up and muscle-bound. Yeah, Lucas saw evil in the man who had bred him.

"Alpha," Lucas said. He never addressed this man as father or dad. He didn't deserve those titles any longer, but his Alpha status couldn't be denied, even by him.

"Where have you been," Marcus sneered at him, "and why are you running through the woods shirtless? You know it isn't safe for you to shift on your own. It isn't allowed."

Lucas wanted to laugh. He had no problem controlling either of his beasts; it was Marcus who wanted him on a leash. At six-foot-four, Lucas towered over the man, but Marcus made him feel small. Lucas knew it was a product of his childhood, but even as an adult, he couldn't completely shake it. Standing there with his arms crossed over his thick chest, Marcus Valentin did what he always did, intimidate. Like a good little solider, Lucas bowed his head, baring his neck; the move always burned him. His otherness fought against it, but it still needed to be done.

"I have done nothing except work for the McClanes as is my duty. The weather is warm, so I removed my shirt, that's all. If there is nothing else Alpha, I would like to retire for the night as is your command. The sun is almost down." Lucas tried to sound contrite, but he knew he failed miserably. Lucas also knew this close to the ceremony, Marcus wouldn't attack him, but it didn't stop the man from putting his hands on him. Marcus grabbed his long hair and pulled his head further to the side.

"Mind yourself, pup. You might be the Guardian, but I am still Alpha, and you will obey."

Lucas gritted his teeth; there was no sense in talking to the man. He had a point to make, and Lucas was sure he would feel that point very soon. Lucas couldn't move his head, but he heard someone clearing their throat.

"Alpha, I need a moment of your time."

Damn, Lucas hated that Flynn was trying to save him because he knew Marcus would take out his anger for Lucas on the man. As he predicted, Marcus released his hair, pushing Lucas away, whirling around to Flynn.

"Omega, what have I told you about interrupting me when I am dealing with my whelp?" Marcus screamed right in the man's face.

Flynn stood his ground; he wasn't a lightweight by any means. Standing just over six-feet and heavily muscled, he was a mountain of a man, but his duty to the pack was to calm and contain the Alpha's fire. Lucas watched as Flynn tried to lay his hand above Marcus' heart, only to have it batted away.

Then Marcus did the unthinkable, reared back and punched the man. Everyone knew if you hurt the Omega, the pain would be returned tenfold. His actions showed just how unstable Marcus had become. Before Marcus could drop to his knees as the fates delivered his punishment, Eric was there to help him move away, leaving Flynn and Lucas laying on the ground.

Lucas stood and brushed himself off, offering Flynn his hand. When Flynn accepted it and hugged him in a manly, side hug, he whispered in his ear.

"You know the time is coming. He is destroying our pack, it is time for you to take your rightful place."

Lucas pulled back and shook his head in denial. He wasn't ready, he didn't feel worthy, and hell, he'd just found Kaylee.

That night, Kaylee tossed and turned; she couldn't get used to being in a new place. Not that her grands home was a new place to her, just different now that she'd been on her own for so long. Then, there was Lucas. She couldn't stop thinking about him. Those blue eyes and that gorgeous, sleek body called to her in a way she had never felt before.

Then there was the dream, that amazing, toe-curling dream. She tried her best to go to sleep and continue it, but she couldn't get her mind to settle. She had so many questions, the top one being, would it really be that good between them? Because, damn, if that was the case, she was more than willing to make that dream a reality. There were others. Why was he here in rural Alabama when he looked like he belonged in a big city? Was he feeling the same things about her she was about him?

Kaylee tossed and turned for hours, changing her night clothes twice because damp panties weren't comfortable. She even went into the bathroom more than a few times to splash cool water on her face. Kaylee even considered digging through her stuff and finding her special little friend, B.O.B. If she weren't under her grandparent's roof right now, she wouldn't have hesitated to relieve some of the tension the dream and Lucas had created in her body.

When the first light of morning started to shine through her window, she gave up and got out of bed. Throwing on a pair of her most comfortable jeans and a ratty t-shirt, Kaylee went into the bathroom and looked in the mirror. She looked like shit. Damn, if the man could cause this much damage after a half hour meeting and a pretty epic dream, she wondered what would happen if she came across him again. Kaylee knew what she would like to happen, she thought, smiling to herself.

Brushing her teeth and throwing her hair up in a messy bun, Kaylee figured this was the best it was going to get today. She didn't feel like messing with makeup or her countless other morning rituals. She was in the country now, it was time to go au naturale, and if someone didn't like it, they could suck it.

She was tired and pissy. All she wanted was a Diet Coke to help lift the fog from her brain and maybe some inside information about Lucas. Going back into the bedroom, Kaylee sat on the bed and put her socks and shoes on, readying herself for the day. Then she made the bed because if Grandma Ruth came up there, she wouldn't be happy if Kaylee left it unmade. Her grandma didn't have many rules, but she liked things tidy.

Living in Birmingham, Kaylee had purposely not made the bed. She could never understand why it was necessary to make it when you were just going to get right back into it later. Here though, Kaylee would make an effort and not complain, well, at least not to anyone. The things she said in her head were all her own; there she could bitch and moan like no other.

Once she opened the door, the smell of burnt bacon and coffee hit her right in the face. Oh lord, her grandma was great at many things, but when she got distracted, watch out. Kaylee often wondered if she didn't get that trait from Grandma Ruth. She could be doing something, a thought or something as simple as a flash of light would distract her, and she would be off to something else.

She was ashamed to admit the Birmingham Fire Department had been at her apartment three times, just this year alone. When she was younger, her Mother took Kaylee and had her tested for ADD. She didn't have it; all the psychological tests had come back negative. The psychologist said she was a daydreamer and needed to focus more on reality.

She remembered that time well. She would see things which were like colors surrounding people; she found out later those were auras, but as a little girl she could only see the colors. She saw how certain people had shadows following them, sometimes another person, other times it was an animal. There was one time when she was in the park, one of the rare occasions her mother had taken off work to spend the day with her, she had to have been about eight at the time. A little boy came up to her, and she asked him about the little puppy following him.

He told her he didn't have a puppy. But Kaylee didn't give up, she pointed to the spot she clearly saw the animal and said, "It's right there." He looked behind himself, looked back at her, and told her she was crazy, there wasn't a puppy there. Kaylee had been determined, not to mention a little stubborn because of her curiosity about the puppy and pointed again, saying, "I'm not crazy, you're crazy because it's your puppy."

The whole thing escalated from there; the little boy started crying and so did Kaylee. His mom and her mother came over and started in on each other. Kaylee tried to explain it to her mother, but she kept saying it wasn't real, there wasn't a puppy, and Kaylee needed to stop saying there was. That wasn't the first time her Mother didn't believe her or take her side.

After what happened at the park, Kaylee was sent here to her grands house. Her Grandma Ruth listened to her and gave her some of her special tea and cookies, but Kaylee couldn't remember what happened next. When she went back home though, the shadows and colors were different, muted somehow, not as distracting, making it easier for her to ignore them. She knew better than to mention them again.

Once she made it to the door of the kitchen, Kaylee leaned up against it and smiled. She loved seeing her Grandma Ruth in here; it wiped out the bad memories and brought on so many good ones. The food might be burnt, but the company was top-notch. Looking at the scene in front of her and remembering many others, she hadn't noticed Grandma Ruth had turned around until she heard her voice.

"Good morning, Kaylee. Take a seat, breakfast is almost ready."

Kaylee knew her hands were clean, but this was another one of Grandma Ruth's rules, everyone washed their hands before sitting at the table. Kaylee walked to the sink to wash her hands like a good granddaughter. Grandma Ruth's smile over her shoulder was reward enough.

Sitting at the little table next to the window, Kaylee enjoyed the crisp, bright colors of the scene outside. Winter was making its way out of the area and Spring was coming. Everything had already started to bloom outside. She loved this time of year.

The view from the window was beautiful, but Kaylee knew if she took a walk outside and around the house, she would see all of her grandma's flower gardens. The woman had a green thumb, something Kaylee hadn't inherited from her. She killed an air plant not too long ago, but she was going to keep that to herself. Not only did Grandma Ruth have multiple flower gardens, she had an herb garden and various fruit trees she tended to. Some of Kaylee's favorite memories were of spending hours out there with her, pulling weeds and talking. Grandma Ruth would explain what each plant and flower was and what they could do. The way she would explain, it was almost like a story.

"Where's Grandpa this morning?" Kaylee asked, getting her head back to the here and now. "I would really like to see him, he wasn't around at all yesterday."

"I think he's down at the cabin with Lucas already. They've been working so hard; you know your Grandpa wants to make it perfect for you, child."

"I know, I was just kind of hoping to see him today," Kaylee said, crestfallen. Her grandpa hadn't come to see her yet. She quickly changed the subject. "So, Lucas? What do you think of him and where did he come from? He doesn't seem like the type of guy to have come from around here."

"He's a hard worker, we've been blessed to have him around. We aren't as spry as we used to be, and he picks up a lot of the chores around this old place. His family lives up the road. He came back to town a couple of months ago."

"So, he's from around here or did the family just move here, too?" Kaylee asked. "I noticed the new house down the road." Kaylee watched as her grandma fidgeted until she turned around and started washing the few dishes left in the sink.

"He used to live here as a child. I'm amazed you two didn't meet before on one of your visits. No matter though, he's a sweet boy, always willing to help, but you need to remember Kaylee, he's working here. You need to let him do his job and stay out of his way."

Okay, Kaylee thought, that statement was weird, and her grandma was acting more bizarre than she'd ever seen, which was saying something. Grandma Ruth was all about southern hospitality. She didn't know Kaylee's thoughts for Lucas were anything beyond being friendly, or did she? Damn, that would be embarrassing. Well, she did call out his name last night, but she had explained that away or at least thought she had. Fuck a duck, no one wanted their grandma knowing they had a crush or more scandalous thoughts about a man.

"I can't wait to go down and see what they've done to the cabin," Kaylee said, changing the subject quickly. "It's been so long since I've even seen the place. I think after breakfast, I'm going to take a walk down there and check it out." Grandma Ruth started to put the food on the table, and Kaylee grabbed a plate.

"Oh, child, let the men be, for now. Edwin will let you know when the cabin is ready, and then you can move right in. I was hoping you would go with me into town today."

Kaylee started to make herself a plate, but after looking at the food, she decided an egg sandwich, minus the burnt to a crisp bacon, was the way to go. After she got the sandwich together, she got up and went to the refrigerator, smiling when she saw the six pack of Diet Coke.

"Sure, I could pick a couple of things up for the cabin while we're there. Where all did you want to go?" Kaylee asked, her back still turned away from her grandma.

"Oh, the usual—the bank, post office, and grocery store. It shouldn't take long."

Kaylee knew better than that. Every time they went to run errands, it took her grandma all day because the woman was a social butterfly. Her family was the only ones who ever got to see the real Ruth McClane—the cantankerous, sarcastic, and blunt woman. Strangers always got the sweet grandmother version; little did they know, she was only out for gossip. Kaylee knew this trip was going to be a pain in her ass, hell, a simple trip to the gas station with her grandma could take an hour, and they were stopping at three places.

Groaning inwardly because she really wasn't feeling up to a day trip to the tiny little town, but didn't want to disappoint her grandma, Kaylee just smiled and agreed. Kaylee wanted to see Lucas again, but if they were in town, and he was working at the cabin that wouldn't happen. Damn, that tall, dark, and handsome man was taking up way too much of her brain space.

She was still bothered by her Grandpa Edwin's absence, and then there was how her grandma responded to any question about Lucas. Her answers were clipped and rushed as if she didn't want to talk about him. That wasn't like her. Grandma Ruth loved to gossip. Kaylee couldn't help feel her Grandma Ruth was trying to caution her away from Lucas. She couldn't figure out why Grandma would let the man work at their home if she didn't trust him with Kaylee. It was like she'd entered the Twilight Zone and her grandma was the same, but different.

Chapter 5

Lucas was out of sorts; his nightly confinement was wearing on him more than it had before. The blood he drank to survive, bagged from a local blood bank, wasn't helping his thirst. In all the years he had been a vampire that hadn't happened to him. The bagged blood provided what he needed, but was never very appealing. He tolerated it, sucking down a bag a night. It held off the hunger enough for him to function. Last night, he had drunk four bags and still felt as though he was starving.

Lucas was an anomaly; he could eat real food, human food, even enjoy it. The difference was it did nothing to nourish his body. When in his wolf form, he could hunt, and his catch for the day would slacken his need; the fresh blood satisfied the vampire and the meat appeased his wolf. But to stay strong, he still had to have human blood. He never drank from the source, it only brought temptation and bloodlust. He had thought he had that need well in control.

With his dual nature, Were and Vampire, it meant death for the person he drank from; it had happened. When he was newly changed, he didn't know what was going on, hadn't learned to control his urges, and had done some horrible things. He refused to let that happen again. That brought to light his newest problem, Kaylee. She was the reason for his current state of discontent.

He wanted her. His beast wanted her, and nothing would curb that need and hunger inside of him. When he was finally able to sleep, he couldn't even escape her there, dreaming of only Kaylee—touching, tasting her skin, and feeding from her veins. He knew what this was; Were lore was clear. When a Were met his mate, they needed to be together, if not physically, then through their dreams until the claim was complete. He took some consolation that Kaylee would be having the same type of dreams about him.

But it didn't help his current state, it was driving him wild with the need to run and feed. There wasn't a shower cold enough anywhere on the planet which would have lessened his arousal. Even taking matters into his own hands had only added to his frustration.

It took him hours of meditation and physical exertion to pull his beast back far enough to leave the pack's home. Flynn's words weighed heavily on him, repeating in his mind over and over again. It was time; Marcus was out of control, he would destroy the pack. Lucas knew all of those things were true, but he couldn't figure out a way to help them. His first and only priority were the McClane's. If he failed in that, he would be put to death.

It was what Marcus was hoping for. That was why Lucas was confined every night and not allowed to shift without supervision. Lucas needed to join with his beast to make himself stronger. All shifters and vampires did, they needed to let their true nature thrive. Lucas knew Marcus was stifling him to make him weak, so when the time came, he would be unable to uphold his duty.

As soon the first rays of light lit the sky, Lucas left his room in the basement. He didn't stick around the pack house to eat and make friendly conversation, he knew they didn't want him there. He chose the solitude of walking in the woods until he was needed at the McClane's house. He hadn't even made it ten steps before his twin made his presence known. After the night Lucas had just had, he really didn't want to deal with his brother.

"Aren't you supposed to be at work or something?"

Matthias sneered at him. Lucas could barely remember a time his twin looked at him with any type of kindness. From the time they were able to comprehend what was going on in the world around them, Marcus had worked his hatred for Lucas into Matthias. Pitting them against each other because of things beyond Lucas' control. Envy, greed, ego, and entitlement tainted them, when they should have been close.

Twin births in the pack were revered. It didn't happen often, and it was said the twins, two sides of one whole, would have more power, strength, and magic than a single birth. If they were Alphas that power would be legendary. He and Matthias were Alphas, only Marcus had severed their bond, making that power useless.

"I saw you yesterday," Matthias stated as if he had just revealed the biggest secret in the world. Lucas didn't play into him; he learned a long time ago if he just waited his brother out, Matt would eventually get to what he really wanted to say.

"Yeah, I saw you too, Matt, kind of hard not to when we live in the same house," Lucas replied as though the conversation meant nothing to him.

"No," Matthias growled, grabbing Lucas' arm, forcing him to turn and face him, "I saw you in the woods yesterday when you shifted."

Lucas knew this was bad, he was forbidden to shift without Marcus present. If Marcus found out, he would be punished, and with Kaylee's ceremony approaching, he couldn't let that happen.

"I don't know what you think you saw Matt, but it wasn't me in my shifted form, I know the rules," Lucas stated without showing a bit of the fear he now felt.

"What I want to know, Guardian, is how you were able to lie to our Alpha without him detecting it," Matthias snarled.

Lucas knew better than to confirm any of Matt's suspicions. Over the years, he had tried to take his brother under his wing and teach him things, so they could rebuild their bond, but it always backfired. Matt would find a way to use anything Lucas showed him against him. Not that it would matter in this instance, Matt could tell Marcus a lie about him, so Lucas would be punished, and the man would swear it was the God's honest truth.

All Shifters had the ability to detect lies, but only a few had the capacity to deceive; Lucas was one of them. He believed it was one of the gifts he received being the Guardian. The gifts were sacred, and he wasn't permitted to share them with anyone, even his brother, so he evaded.

"I don't know what you're talking about, Matt. I'm not able to lie to Marcus anymore than you or any member of the pack."

"See, that's just the thing. I know you just lied through your teeth, yet none of my senses picked up on your deception. I want to know how you do it, otherwise, I'll be informing our Alpha of your little tromp through the woods in wolf form yesterday."

"Don't threaten me, Matt, it will get you nowhere," Lucas growled back, his wolf riding him to attack.

"That might be true, Lucas, but I'm sure the photos I took on my phone will provide me with proof enough to give to our Alpha. Of course, if you're willing to tell me, we could always avoid that."

"What's your deal?" Lucas yelled, pulling away from Matt's grip. "Do you even pay attention to what Marcus is doing to the pack, do you care? Or are you so blinded by your dedication and devotion to our father you can't see what's right in front of your face?"

"You don't know what you're talking about, Lucas. You're the one who doesn't pay attention to the pack's needs. It's all about your guardianship. You come only when required. You don't see the struggle our Alpha goes through just to keep a roof over our heads and food on the table. You're the selfish one, not our father," Matt sneered.

"Really, brother, I never once, until this moment, thought you were naïve. The Council pays for the pack house, and all packs in the area provide a stipend to our pack because of my status as Guardian. Marcus is using the money for something other than the pack. If you don't believe me, contact the Council, it's all public information, including the amount each pack provides every month," Lucas said.

"That's not true. You're lying again. Our Alpha would never do that. The pack and its wellbeing come first, in all things. Those are his teachings. I will not be turned by your lies," Matt screamed.

Lucas had enough, he didn't want to play this game with Matt anymore, so he challenged.

"Believe what you want, but think about this while you're packing up groceries at your job at the Piggly Wiggly; it isn't needed. The Valentin pack is provided for so we're available to the McClanes at all times. All you have to do is make one simple phone call to confirm it. Do you have the balls to go against everything our father has taught you and think for yourself for once in your life? Or do you want to remain clueless as well as penniless while he reaps the rewards of the Council, outlying packs, and the blood sweat and tears of our own?"

Lucas' statements had the desired effect; he watched Matt storm away. Lucas waited because he knew, just like his father, Matt always had to have the last word, and he didn't make him wait long.

"I will prove you the liar you are, Lucas, make no mistake. When I do, I'll take all of this—your shift, your lies against him and the packs—to our father, and you'll be punished."

Lucas started walking, but needed to say one more thing. There would always be a part of him which hoped he could get through Marcus' lies and reach Matt.

"I believe you are the one who is about to learn some hard truths about the man you hold so dear. What will you do with the answers?"

Lucas hadn't raised his voice or even turned to face his brother. Their Shifter hearing was impeccable, he knew he had heard him, only this time Matt didn't respond. In Lucas' book that was a victory.

Lucas continued his journey through the woods; his earlier agitation amplified by his confrontation with his brother. The cabin for Kaylee was almost done, but he knew she would need firewood to stave off the cold winter months to come. It would also calm his beasts and his mind.

When he broke through woods into the clearing, Edwin was waiting for him on the porch. The man wasn't usually at the cabin until after ten in the morning. His being here now concerned Lucas. He walked a little faster because he knew something was wrong.

"Is there a problem? Is Kaylee okay?"

"That's the problem, Guardian, your concern over my granddaughter. You are only to concern yourself with her safety after she has come into her magic. As she has yet to complete the Ostara, you're not needed. Her wellbeing will always be a matter for her family and mate. That isn't you, Lucas Valentin; the Guardian and the Blue Moon Priestess are never to be mates."

"Old man, I have read the bylaws and the history regarding my station, and you are incorrect in your beliefs, but I won't stand in your way as of now. My purpose is to ensure the ceremony goes off without a hitch and your granddaughter comes into her powers. I will do that, but make no mistake, if we are mates, then I will claim her. There isn't anything you or anyone else can say or do to prevent that, do you understand?"

Lucas hated using his power against people. Edwin was a warlock, but a weak one; Ruth was the one with all the power. It was her line which provided the next generation of witches. Edwin was her chosen mate, but not her only one. Ruth had other children, children who wouldn't be revealed to Kaylee until the ceremony. Just like her mother before her, Kaylee would soon find out her family's origin and that it was much larger than she ever thought. Lucas knew this because part of his job as Guardian was to keep and guard the McClane's family tree. Edwin knew as well and even though Lucas genuinely liked the old man, he was meddling in places he shouldn't.

"We'll see about that." Edwin got up and left the porch, but looked back at Lucas. "If Ruth decides there will be no mating between the two of you, it will not happen. I promise you, half breed, I will do my very best to convince her the mating is tainted because you are not of pure blood."

"If I know anything of your mate, old man, it's that she doesn't mess with fate. You might want to remember that while you're doing your best to convince her of something which hasn't happened yet or might not ever happen. I have been loyal to the McClane's from birth. I take that duty seriously, and will remain doing it until my dying breath, guardianship or not. My blood has nothing to do with that, it only makes me work harder."

Chapter 6

Kaylee felt like a ten-year-old shuffling out to the car, but damn, she didn't want to do this. Shopping and errands were fun if you could get something nice, like a great pair of jeans or even a killer pair of heels. But going to the grocery store with her grandma, yeah, that would never be on her top ten things to do in a day, heck, maybe in a year.

That reminded her of another thing; who in their right mind named a grocery store after a wiggling pig? The Piggly Wiggly!! Then plaster pictures of said pig with a huge smile on its face, wearing a butcher's hat. How was a person supposed to buy yummy breakfast meats like bacon, sausage, or ham with that damn pig smiling at them? Or, heck, how about pork chops? That pig made Kaylee feel guilty, so she always steered clear of the pork products, and it pissed her off.

A girl needed some bacon, every once in a while, or a nice, juicy pork chop. But, no, the Wiggly had ruined that for her. Kaylee never felt these things in Birmingham at Kroger's or Winn Dixie. She could snap up pork products and anything else she wanted, left and right, with absolutely no guilt. Well, maybe a little guilt on those days she decided on a junk food binge, but that was the store's fault.

No, this honor was just for the Piggly Wiggly in good old Eclectic. It was the only grocery store around unless you wanted to drive even further; Kaylee didn't. The drive was another reason she was dragging her feet. She knew her Grandma Ruth was going to want to drive, and the woman was a terror on the roads.

She drove with two feet, but the left one only got action when a stop sign, another car, or heck, a person was within six feet of the front of the car. When that happened, she slammed that foot down like nobody's business. The right foot, now that baby got a lot of play, as in pushed down to the floor from the moment the car was started up.

Forget about the front, walking behind Grandma Ruth's car was taking your life in your hands. She didn't look when she backed up; if you were unfortunate enough be behind her, she deemed it was your responsibility, not hers. Kaylee had witnessed her saying just that years ago when she ran right into a police cruiser. Kaylee had been about fourteen at the time and remembered the cop looking at Grandma Ruth like she was nuts. Kaylee agreed on some level, quite a few of them, actually.

That was when an idea hit her. She hadn't been back here much since she'd gotten her driver's license or had her own car. Grandma Ruth usually visited her in Birmingham during the years since her mom moved to California. The more she thought about, the more a plan came together in her head. She decided to go for broke, right before her grandma got to her car.

"Grandma Ruth, why don't I drive this time? I didn't get a chance to fill up yesterday before I got here and would like to top off the gas tank," Kaylee said smiling, trying to look as sweet and innocent as possible. She should have known it wouldn't work.

"Oh, Kaylee, there isn't any need for that," Grandma Ruth said, holding her hand in the air, complete with jingling keys. "If you have to go somewhere, we'll just take you. Why spend money when you don't need to? You have to remember, you don't have a job, right now, which means you're going to have to watch your pocketbook."

Yeah, Kaylee knew she needed to watch her spending, but filling up her gas tank wasn't going to exactly break the bank. But it did bring up another problem; Kaylee needed a job. She had enough savings to get through a couple of months, maybe. Not having to pay rent would help, but she would still have to pay for utilities and food. Kaylee stopped walking when she realized Grandma Ruth had turned and was talking to her.

"Kids your age are too frivolous. Things are too easy come, easy go for you youngins. Why, I remember having the same pair of shoes for two years, wore them every day walking to and from school. Now, people have rooms just filled with only shoes."

All Kaylee could do was stare at her grandma, then, suppressing her giggle, she asked, "Was that when you lived in the Bayou? I thought you told me you had to paddle your johnboat for two hours just to get to school and your family was so poor you couldn't afford things like shoes?"

Her grandma didn't miss a beat, waving her keychain-clad hand in the air and said like it was just common sense, "Oh, that was another time. I did go to school for eight years, Kaylee. It's not like all of them were the same, you know. That's another thing about you kids, always trying to rush things."

This time Kaylee did giggle, "Of course Grandma, whatever you say."

When they rounded the corner of the garage, Kaylee froze in place, looking at her grandma's car and again considered trying to come up with something, anything which would make the woman let her drive because what was before her now couldn't be safe. The pink—yes pink, but not just pink, day-glow pink—late model Cadillac sedan was a tank and had more than a few problems.

The first one, from what Kaylee could see, was the car didn't have any hubcaps. No big deal, but then there were the side panels. Those looked like someone beat the car with a hammer. And the bumper or lack of one; someone had fashioned a two-by-four where the bumper should be and on it were a couple of placards like you would see on semis or work vehicles.

One said, This vehicle takes wide turns. The next said, This vehicle stops frequently, and in marker across the bottom, it included, quickly. But the one which caught Kaylee's eye was a huge hand-painted one which said, If you can read this, you are too close. Kaylee was pretty sure anyone within a hundred feet of the car could have read the sign. Which said a lot about her grandma's driving skills or lack of them.

"Grandma what's with all the bumper stickers? You do know they're supposed to go on the back of the car, right?"

"Oh, those. Your grandpa said if I banged up the car again, he was going to take my keys away. Those sticker things distract him, and I get to keep my keys. Did you see the one that says, Horn's broke watch for fingers? He loves that one. Shook his head and laughed for a good half hour. Which reminds me, we're going to need to make a stop at the police station." Her grandma said it like it was an everyday occurrence and no big deal.

"Uh, Gram, why do we need to stop at the police station?"

"Do you remember the nice officer who put his cruiser in the wrong place and my car hit him? He gives me more stickers when I come in to pay my tickets. Such a nice man. He's the one who helped with my new bumper. Even gave me the signs."

Kaylee was too stunned to say anything but "Oh."

As Grandma Ruth opened her door, it screeched with the sound of metal against metal, making Kaylee grit her teeth. Walking to her side of the car, she cringed a little when opening her door resulted in the same noise. Getting in, she quickly put her seat belt on, just in time for her grandma to put the pedal to the metal and tear out of the driveway.

Kaylee couldn't look out the windshield. She'd made that mistake once, and her foot had slammed on an imaginary brake pedal. That only left her with two choices; she could either watch her hands as her knuckles got whiter with the grip she had on both the armrest and the seat, or she could look out of the side window. She chose the latter.

Her grandma was always surprisingly quiet as she drove. It was like she was on a mission, and Kaylee wasn't about to distract her in any way. The thirty-minute drive to Eclectic took her grandma eighteen. Kaylee looked around; the town of Eclectic was nothing but a one-traffic light, one-road town. Kaylee knew from her conversations with her grandma, the most exciting news going around right now was the new Dollar General being built. Oh, how exciting… not. If a McDonalds or a Starbucks was going in, she would have been right on the excitement bandwagon. But a Dollar General? Not so much.

By the time they pulled into the grocery store, Kaylee was more than ready to be out of the car. Once on solid ground, she had to resist the urge to kiss the pavement or offer her thanks to a higher being for getting her there in one piece.

Damn, this place hadn't changed since she was a child. The store had been in Eclectic for fifty or more years. At least, that's what the sign next to the door said. It was crowded; being the only grocery store in town or within a thirty-mile radius, everyone shopped here. It was also one of the biggest employers in the area and where she would probably be working if she couldn't find something else. She didn't have a lot of faith in finding something else. Needing a break from her grandma, Kaylee got her own cart, one with a wobbly wheel, of course.

"Grandma I'm going to go pick up a few things. When do you want to meet back up at the front, so we can check out together?"

"I only have a few things to get. How does an hour sound?"

"Okay, meet you back here in an hour." Kaylee wanted to groan again or roll her eyes, she wasn't sure which expression was the most appropriate. She knew she would be sitting out front, all her shopping done, well before her grandma even if she walked slow and read every label on the products she picked up and all the magazines by the cash register.

Kaylee had been wandering around the store forever, fighting her wobbly cart every inch of the way when she remembered she needed to get one more thing. She was about to pick up some tampons when she got distracted by the 'adult' section located right next to the feminine products section. Thinking about her dreams last night and Lucas, she picked up two packages of condoms and started reading the back. A girl could never be too prepared after all.

Then she noticed it in all its promised glory, 'the pleasure pack'. She grabbed the box and almost started to do a little dance—the words twisted, sensations, intense, and warming all made her mind drift to a certain man. She started looking all over the box for a size; didn't they have sizes?

"Can I help you, Kaylee?" an intensely deep, but gruff, and somewhat familiar voice spoke very close to her ear.

Kaylee dropped the box and spun around. At first, she thought the man standing in front of her was Lucas, but then she noticed several things; his eyes were green and his hair was much shorter. The biggest difference, she didn't feel anything but mild appreciation for this man. No belly flutters, hard nipples, or wet panties. He was hot, hell, he was a mirror image of Lucas, but he wasn't him.

"How do you know who I am, but I haven't got the first clue who you are?" Kaylee asked. Something was putting her off this man. It wasn't fear or trepidation, it was more like anger. She felt it coming off him in waves, not directed at her exactly, but someone close to her. Kaylee never could explain how she felt other people's feelings, she just did. It was instinct or self-preservation, she didn't know and hadn't or wouldn't talk to anyone about it.

"The name is Matthias." The man looked at her and smiled a little too broad and a lot too toothy. "Lucas told me all about you, Kaylee."

The way he said Lucas told me all about you rubbed her the wrong way. He sounded as if he was implying something she was sure she wouldn't like. The damn eyebrow bob thing he did only confirmed it.

"Nice to meet you, Matthias. Care to share exactly what Lucas told you about me?" Kaylee didn't take the hand Matt had offered to her.

She knew it was rude, but she didn't want to touch him, so she crossed her arms over her chest and waited to hear what he had to say about Lucas.

"Oh, by the looks of what you're interested in buying, I think you know. Didn't take him long. I heard you've only been in town for one night. You have to be his fastest conquest, yet. But I wouldn't bother buying those. Lucas is a one and done type of guy. Unless, you'd consider taking me for a spin. I like to sample the new pieces for a long while," Matt said with half laden eyes, licking his lips.

"Really? Well, that's good to know, and I think I changed my mind," Kaylee said, picking up the box of condoms and slamming them down on the shelf. How dare he, how dare both of them? Kaylee wasn't a virgin, but she wasn't easy either. Lucas Valentin could kiss her ass if he was going around saying she was. As for Matt, he could kiss her ass just for being a douche.

Kaylee went right to the cash registers and checked out. Thankfully, Grandma Ruth was making her way up to the registers as well. Once they both walked out of the store, Kaylee helped her grandma load up her groceries, then grabbed her grandma's keys.

"I'm driving home."

Her grandma must have noticed her mood because she didn't say a word, just got in the car. Kaylee followed suit, keeping quiet as she brooded about Lucas. When she got back to the house, she was going to find the bastard and the two of them were going to straighten some things out, right from the start. If she was going to be called a slut, then she'd better have done the acts to deserve the title.

Chapter 7

Kaylee was tired, frustrated and angry, well, not just angry, she was downright pissed. How dare Lucas talk about her that way? They didn't know each other, and he sure as hell couldn't see into her mind, so he had no idea she'd one of the best sex dreams of her life starring him. Even then, he still had no right to imply she had slept with him or done anything.

Kaylee had fumed the entire way home thinking about it. When they got there, Kaylee hastily helped her grandma put away the groceries. Well, put away was a loose way of saying she threw, stuffed, and crammed things where she thought they should go. She shouldn't have, she should have taken more care, but she was just too damn mad.

Her Grandma Ruth had been quiet the entire way home and even as Kaylee sort of helped. When Kaylee slammed the last cupboard door and said, "I'm going for a walk," her grandma still didn't say anything. When Kaylee went out the door and slammed it, too, still nothing. She should be ashamed of herself, Matthias's words shouldn't have upset her this much. Normally, they wouldn't have; she would have put him in his place and been on her way. But this was Lucas they were talking about, and the words hurt her more than they should have. The same man she had these weird feelings for, the same man who was so sweet to her yesterday, how could he be a douchebag, too?

Kaylee didn't consider herself to be naïve, she had met and even dated her fair share of assholes. She also knew anybody was capable of anything, even lying to make themselves look better in front of their friends. Kaylee just wasn't that type of person. She believed being honest was the only way to go. Even little white lies had a way of coming back to haunt you. Now, lies by omission, she didn't believe those were lies at all, a person should be able to keep some things to themselves. But if Lucas said he'd fucked her, it was a whopper lie which needed punishment or retribution. She wasn't beyond doing either to Lucas.

Kaylee decided walking to the cabin would be better for everyone involved. The fresh air might calm her down a little, which was doubtful, but one could hope, and she needed the extra time the walk would take just to process everything. If she got in the car, it would take her less than two minutes to get there; this way, it would take her at least fifteen.

The well-worn path was right next to the shed, and Kaylee had been down it tons of times as a child, so she wasn't worried about getting lost. She had been walking for a while, caught up in all her nasty thoughts of what she was going to do to Lucas, when someone screamed, "Boo!" behind her. Kaylee didn't even think, she balled up her fist and rounded on whoever the hell it was in a move which would have made her self-defense teacher proud and planted her fist right in the person's face.

It took her mind a second to figure out what was going on, but once it caught up, she considered tackling the person and repeating her impressive punch. When he looked up and glared at her, Kaylee knew exactly who it was.

"What the hell, Matthias! Where did you come from and how in the heck did you make it out here before me? Weren't you working?" Kaylee asked.

He looked at her all stunned and shocked and roared with a bit of a growl mixed in, "You punched me!"

"And that surprises you, why? A woman walking in the woods by herself and a stranger yells boo, coming out from who knows where, and you thought you would what? Get away with it? Get a good laugh by making me scream? Well, let me tell you something, Matthias Valentin, I don't work that way. Now, go away. I have had enough of you to last a lifetime.

"Kaylee, wait. Listen, I'm sorry, you're right, I did think it would be funny to make you scream, but I needed to talk to you."

Kaylee stood there looking down at Matthias who decided to look pathetic with little puppy dog eyes and a slight pout of his lower lip. Kaylee gave up the fight. She had punched him, which he deserved, the least she could do was hear him out. She crossed her arms under her breast and tapped her foot to show him he only had so much time to say whatever it was he needed to say, so he better get on with it. The problem with that was as soon as she crossed her arms, the jerkwad started staring at her boobs, his mouth hanging open.

"Matt." Kaylee said. When that didn't work, she repeated it just a little louder, "Matt!" When he still seemed to be entranced by her boobs, she finally screamed, "Matthias!" She watched as he seemed to shake himself out of whatever he'd been thinking about, but he was still looking at her boobs. Yeah, it was kind of flattering, but still creepy.

"My face is up here, Matthias," Kaylee stated drolly.

"Yeah, I know, but I think my eyes like where they're looking, better," Matt responded, but didn't move his eyes one fraction of a millimeter.

"How about I explain it another way for the short bus boy? You better look up here at my face, so you can say what you want, or I will punch you again, and this time, I will make sure you can't see out of both your eyes because they will be swollen shut. If that isn't convincing enough, I will also be kicking you in the balls while I'm landing the punches," Kaylee explained.

At the mention of the word balls, Matt's eyes snapped right to hers, and he cupped himself as if she was going to do it any second. Kaylee wasn't sure, she still might if he kept this crap up. Matt stood up and stepped away from her, another good move. He also kept his eyes on either her face or her feet.

"Fine, I wanted to talk to you about Lucas. What I said back there at the grocery store wasn't true. So, I left and followed you here. Girl you drive like a freaking grandma, by the way.

"I do not," Kaylee screamed, throwing her hands in the air. "Have you seen the way my grandma drives?"

"Point taken," Matt said, shrugging his shoulders. "Anyway, Lucas pissed me off this morning, and I knew he had a thing for you. I wanted to pay him back by pissing you off, so you would stay away from him."

"How old are you?"

"Twenty-seven."

"And you're still playing little high school games? I mean, seriously, I'm only twenty-four, and even I wouldn't do that shit. What did he do to piss you off, and how did you even know about me?"

"I know about you because we're neighbors. My family lives right up the road. Shit, even you should know anyone new in this fucking little town is on everyone's radar. Plus, Ruth and Edwin have been talking about you coming for a few weeks now."

"You know my grandparents?"

"Yeah, like I said, we're neighbors, plus, my brother works for them, so...."

"Yeah, I get it, stupid question. Now tell me what Lucas did to piss you off."

"Family shit, mostly. He lied to our dad and then refused to tell me something."

"Again, you're twenty-seven? Not twelve?"

Matt smiled a genuine smile, and it softened him. She also wasn't getting the angry vibe from him anymore.

"So, what changed why are you coming clean to me now?" she asked. "Why not just keep me pissed and away from Lucas? You would have won that way."

"He made me face the truth about a few things, so I thought I would return the favor. Nothing else."

"So, you aren't going to tell me exactly what he said, how he lied, or what he made you see?" Matt smiled and shook his head. "Okay, then keep your secrets. I'm heading to my cabin. You want to tag along? I think Lucas is still there. Maybe you two need to talk more than I need to speak with him."

"No, I need to get back, my family will be waiting on me for dinner."

Kaylee punched Matt in the arm. When he rubbed it and looked at her like she was nuts, Kaylee said, "You're married with kids and you still hit on me? How dare you!"

"Huh, what are you talking about married and kids? Oh, my family, no, my Dad and a few other family members, not as in my wife and kids, but my family," Matt explained.

"Okay, so why isn't Lucas going to your 'family' dinner?" Kaylee asked.

"He wasn't invited because he is an epic asshole most days, and I still think you should pick me over him," Matt sneered.

"I'm not picking either of you," Kaylee laughed. "Why do you still live with your Dad and brother?"

"Why do you live with your grandparents?" Matt barked, seemingly annoyed by her question.

She didn't care, she was curious, and he was the one who owed her.

"I don't. I'm staying with them until the cabin is ready. Once it is, I'll be living there by myself."

"Yeah, well it's just easier to stay with the pack. That way we can all help each other out if needed."

"But not Lucas?"

"No, not Lucas. Okay, listen, I have to go. Next time we talk, how about we keep Lucas out of it?"

"You're the one who brought him up in the first place."

"Whatever. Bye, Kaylee."

"Bye, Matthias, it wasn't as bad talking to you this time. Have fun with the family."

When Kaylee turned around and saw her grandpa standing a little way down the trail, she couldn't help it any more than when she saw her grandma yesterday. She ran to him, hugging him tight.

"Why have you been hiding from me?

"Kaylee, girl, I haven't been hiding, just trying to get the cabin ready for you, hon," her grandpa said, placing a kiss on her forehead.

"Well, it felt like you were hiding, you old coot. I didn't get to see you at dinner last night or this morning for breakfast, and I missed you," Kaylee said pouting.

"None of that now, sweet girl." Her grandpa tweaked her nose and said, "How about we go down to the cabin, so you can see what's been keeping me so busy? It's almost ready for you to move in."

"I would love that," Kaylee agreed. Taking his arm, they walked to the cabin, talking and catching up. Kaylee loved both her grands, but Grandpa held a special place in her heart. When the cabin finally came into view, all Kaylee could say was, "Wow." The cabin looked nothing like she remembered. The log walls had been pressure washed and sealed, making them shine with a beautiful orange tone.

Then there was the porch; it hadn't been there before at all. The posts holding up it up looked like they had been made from some of the beautiful fir trees which decorated the surrounding land, just like the main house. Those too had been stained and sealed, so they shined to match the walls of the cabin. The floor and steps were painted a hunter green. White rocking chairs and a swing decorated the porch, making it even more inviting. Kaylee could see herself spending a lot of time out there.

Kaylee kept looking and was delighted by every new detail. Cedar planked the roof, but the real focal point was the front door. It was simply gorgeous with stained glass panels and carved, dark wood framing. She knew her grandpa had to have gotten it from the local antique shop. It looked like something a person would find in a luxury home, not in rural Alabama. Kaylee took a couple of minutes just to run her hand over it before opening it to explore the inside of the cabin.

The inside was tiny, but cozy. The darker beams and cedar ceiling drew her eyes like a moth to a flame. The floor plan was simple, but exactly what Kaylee had always wanted—a living room with a massive stone fireplace, kitchen with a small island, and two doors which were currently closed. She knew one held the only bathroom and the other was a closet. There was a staircase in the middle, leading to a loft space and the only bedroom.

She had always liked the cabin, but now it felt like it was hers, every improvement had been made with her in mind. Like the two huge windows on either side of the fireplace. She might have liked the cabin, but she absolutely loved the pond, and her grandpa knew that, so he gave her the ability to see it as much as she wanted. Water had always soothed her; if she was in a panic, just looking at a body of water—lake, pond, river, creek, or ocean—would instantly put her at ease. Now, she had that right inside her new home. Turning to her grandpa, she hugged him again and started to cry.

"Thank you so much for this."

"This place is special, Kaylee girl, just like you are. How about I leave you here for a little while, so you can get acquainted with your new home?" Grandpa said as he was walking out the door. He never was very good with her crying; she knew he would head back home to tell Grandma Ruth about it, so she could fix it. That made Kaylee smile and cry a little more.

Chapter 8

After her grandpa left, Kaylee walked around the cabin, touching things, getting a feel for the place. Her grands had done so much for her, there were little touches all over the place. Like the dark leather couch which looked so comfy and soft, she couldn't resist sitting on it for a second to feel it against her body; she wasn't disappointed. Kaylee could see herself lounging, watching tv, reading a book, or heck, sleeping on it under the amazing hand-knitted afghan draped across the back.

Clutching a corner of the afghan, she brought it to her nose and knew right away her grandma had made it just for her. Getting up, she tested out the leather recliner which matched the couch and was just as nice. The area rug was old, more than likely antique; she was sure it was another one of her grandpa's touches. It had multiple earth tones and matched the cabin's decor perfectly, as far as Kaylee was concerned; a little eclectic and a lot shabby chic, just her style. It also provided a place in front of the fireplace for her to set up camp and ward off the cold winters nights.

But it was the windows and what was behind them which kept drawing her eye. Walking closer to the window, she looked out at the pond. The water's surface was smooth and glistening in the sun, but for the first time in her life, it wasn't the water that soothed her, it was the man chopping wood. Kaylee didn't need to see his face, her body knew it was Lucas. Parts of her got heavy, others turned liquid. The gargantuan butterflies dancing in her stomach and the faster beat of her heart confirmed it.

She no longer felt the need to confront him because Matt had explained what happened and why he said the things he did, so she watched, like a stalker observing her prey. Gorgeous wasn't a strong enough word to describe him. Hell, with his shirt off, Kaylee was having problems moving her eyes away from his washboard abs and those amazing notches framing his well-defined, eight-pack and a happy trail she desperately wanted to explore.

Kaylee thought someone once told her it was called the Adonis belt and the name fit because Lucas had a body of a god; the rest of him wasn't too bad either. Kaylee could spend hours just watching him move. The way his muscles flexed and contracted caused a few contractions within her own body.

Then there was his hair. Kaylee had never once been jealous of a man's hair. Right now, it was in a man bun, which was super-hot, but Kaylee knew from yesterday, when it was free, his silky locks were long and lush. Her fingers twitched to get a handful, so she could pull him close for the kiss she craved.

His face, damn, it was a piece of art all on its own—bright blue eyes, supple suckable lips, and... Oh Shit, he was looking at her, smiling. Damn it, would she ever be able to look at this man without making a fool of herself? She decided it was probably best to go out there and actually say a few words instead of staring at him like some kind of creeper. Kaylee went to the back door and was greeted with the most deliciously deep voice.

"Hi, Kaylee."

Kaylee didn't talk, only waved like a complete dork because she was suddenly tongue-tied. He was leaning against the ax handle, looking at her like she was his next meal; Kaylee was all for it.

"So, what do you think about your cabin? Your grandparents did it up right, I think?"

Clearing her throat and swallowing the mouthful of drool, Kaylee smiled shyly, looking down at her feet and said, "Yeah, I really like it." She was twenty-four, but just the sight of Lucas made her feel like a high school teen staring at her first crush.

Kaylee wanted to run back to the cabin and get a clue or hide her face in a pillow and scream. Why couldn't she talk to this man? Hell, she'd spoken to his brother just fine, even yelled at him, but every time Lucas was around, she seemed to be missing brain cells.

"So, you should be ready to move in a few days. Are you excited?"

Kaylee gathered up every nerve she had and said, "I can't wait. I'm so glad it's not going to be as long as I thought. When I talked to my grands last week, they said it could take up to a month more." Lucas laughed, and Kaylee melted. The sound did things to her even more than his voice did. It also made her want to go all girly and giggly.

"Hey, you want to take a walk around the pond with me?" Lucas asked.

Kaylee finally found her voice, and with a slight smile on her lips, her eyes peeking through her lashes, and of course, blushing like nobody's business, Kaylee said, "Yeah sure why not." Like his request was no big deal, something she did every day, when the truth was him wanting to spend time with her at the pond meant everything to her.

Kaylee wasn't a shy girl, but Lucas made her feel that way. Well, until her brain decided to say something really inappropriate. Lucas went to grab his shirt when Kaylee blurted out.

"Oh, you don't have to put it on because of me. I kind of like the view without it." Kaylee wanted to kick her damn self, but Lucas saved her again, laughing it off.

"Damn, I think I'll have to walk around half-naked more often if it gets that pretty color on your cheeks."

"You can't be serious. What woman wouldn't like to look at you like this, Lucas?" Kaylee said while waving her hand in front of her face to emphasize her point. "You do know how incredibly hot you are, right? I mean just look at your abs. Hell, not just those—your pecs, that chest, your eight-pack, the tattoos. Oh, my gawd, you are every woman's wet dream or at least a big percentage of them!" Kaylee exclaimed.

Lucas smiled, and completely serious, whispered, "I don't want to be every woman's wet dream, Kaylee, just one woman's."

Kaylee knew he was talking about her. She wanted to jump up and down, doing a happy dance to end all happy dances, but refrained and kept smiling. Her motor mouth stayed shut, for once.

"Come on, let's go for that walk."

When he held out his hand to her, Kaylee took it without a second thought. It seemed and felt incredibly natural to touch and be around him. About halfway around the pond, Kaylee spotted a bench. She knew her grandpa had done that too. Pulling Lucas, she didn't stop until they made it there. Kaylee sat down, not giving Lucas any choice but to join her because she hadn't let go of his hand, and didn't plan to anytime soon. She stared at the water for a little while, feeling the shyness creeping back in, and could feel Lucas staring at her.

"I ran into your brother today." The grip he had on her hand tightened, and in her peripheral vision, she could see his body straighten until he was almost rigid with tension. She ran her thumb over his hand in soothing circles, and it must have worked because he relaxed slightly.

"You met Matthias today?" Lucas groaned. "Did he say anything about me?"

"Actually, that's what was kind of weird. He did say a bunch of shit about you, but then took it all back. He informed me you told him you fucked me, and he also clued me in on the fact you were a one and done type of guy," Kaylee said.

"I'm going to kill him," Lucas said through gritted teeth. Kaylee continued to move her thumb over his hand and leaned her head against his shoulder.

"Listen, Lucas, honestly, it's okay. He said he was mad at you, but then felt bad, so he made sure I knew he'd lied. It's not a big deal."

"That's just it, Kaylee, it is a big deal, my family," he paused, and Kaylee felt his head tip back, looking to the sky for the words he needed, then he huffed and continued, "I don't really get along with them, and they aren't thrilled I'm back living under the same roof."

"What do you, I mean why do you live with them? I know my grands can't be paying you much, but can't you get a place of your own?" Kaylee asked. "Just looking at the cabin, I know you have amazing carpentry skills. My Grandpa Edwin wouldn't know a screwdriver from a hammer."

She really wanted to know. She was twenty-four and had been living on her own since she was eighteen when her mom moved back to California. She wasn't judging him, hell, she'd moved to live in a cabin her grandparents provided, but she was still living there and paying the utilities on her own.

"It's not about money or not having work. I have a job, two of them; it's why I'm here, right now, and living with my family. Once the job is over, I'll be moving on and out. I just can't do that right now, which really sucks because the longer I stay there, the less I want to. Matt is alright, but spoiled, and my Father, that man is a right bastard on a good day," Lucas explained.

"I'm sorry to hear that. I was an only child and my parents weren't together. I don't know my father, but as soon as I turned eighteen, my mother left me for greener pastures. She was never mean, maybe a little dismissive and a bit too selfish, but never mean. What other job do you have?" Kaylee asked.

"Kaylee, I'm sorry, I can't talk about it, right now, but I promise, one day I will. Can you give me that?" Lucas asked, turning slightly making Kaylee pick up her head, so she could look him in the eyes. Before she could give him an answer, he said, "Damn you are so beautiful, Kaylee." Lucas used his hand to brush her somewhat curly blonde hair off of her face and over her shoulder, brushing his fingertips first over her cheek, then down her neck to her shoulder, causing tingles to erupt all over Kaylee's body.

When he picked up the end and quirked his eyebrow, Kaylee smiled and said, "I like to be original" and shrugged her shoulders. She had dyed the tips purple before she moved. It had been something she'd always wanted to do, but couldn't while working at the bank.

"I like it. It fits you, somehow," Lucas said, smiling at the lock of hair in question.

"Thank you, Lucas." Kaylee could feel the heat on her cheeks and knew she was blushing again, but the blush had nothing to do with the compliment he just gave her. She was sitting there debating whether she should let her inner bad girl out to play. She wanted to do more than sit there holding hands. It was nice, sweet even, but she was dying to feel his lips on hers.

It looked like she and Lucas were on the same page because he brought his hand back up from her shoulder, gliding it over the side of her neck, cupping the back of her neck, and pulling her as close as she could get. Kaylee didn't hesitate, kissing him softly, at first, then cocking her head, opening her mouth a little, and running her tongue along his lower lip.

That was all it took for Lucas to take over. His lips covered hers as his tongue plunged deep, swirling around hers, tasting, exploring. The kiss quickly turned heated. Kaylee straddled his lap, grinding herself against him, and he started thrusting his tongue in and out of her mouth like he was fucking her, lifting his hips when she pushed down; Kaylee moaned. She hated the clothes covering their bodies, longed to feel his skin against her own.

Kaylee felt a slight pinch of pain when his tooth caught her lip, but it only added to the ferocity of the kiss, making her hotter. She tried to show him with the kiss, but Lucas picked her up, breaking their connection and sat her down on the bench. He didn't waste a single minute, getting up and running toward the woods and the trail.

Confused and hurt, she screamed his name. He continued to run, but looked over his shoulder at her, his face tense, his lips drawn in a straight line, but damn, why were his eyes glowing a copper color. Why wasn't it scaring the ever-loving hell out of her?

Chapter 9

Lucas barely made it out of Kaylee's line of sight, and his beasts were clawing at him to change. This wasn't his usual change into his wolf, this one was different, and Lucas was fighting it with everything he had in him. His beasts, the vampire and the wolf, had combined and were driving him to go back to Kaylee, his mate, their mate.

Lucas wouldn't, couldn't let that happen. This beast was bigger, stronger, and deadlier, but what scared him the most and made him fight harder to maintain his human form was this beast was also uncontrollable; it took over his body and mind completely. The pain of fighting it back was unbelievable. Lucas staggered, falling to his knees, but he needed to get away from Kaylee, so he forced his changing body to move.

He only made it a few more steps when he fell into a tree, breathing heavily. This wouldn't work, Lucas needed to get further away, but his body wasn't cooperating with him. He couldn't let the beasts out. That was when he smelled him, Matt. Looking up, he saw him standing not too far away. Lucas growled and snarled, the animal was wanting to attack his brother for being so close to his mate, but he fought and managed to say in a more animalistic than a human voice, "Get help."

Lucas knew just saying those two words could get him killed. If Marcus came, Lucas knew he would use this shift as a reason to eliminate him. Hell, he was even okay with it as long as Kaylee remained safe. Safe from him.

That burned. He was supposed to protect her and her family and because of one mistake years before, he was going to fail. The taste of her blood was still on his lips, driving the vampire and wolf crazy, in his mind and body.

One drop of her blood had produced a bloodlust stronger than Lucas had ever experienced before, even during his transition. This was different, stronger, more potent. Bringing his hands up, Lucas tried to remove his shirt. The skin beneath it was burning with the fur of his beast. It felt as though each and every one of his pores was on fire and the fabric was abrading his skin. His claws had descended, making the task near impossible. Lucas gave up trying and just ripped the fucker off and started to crawl.

If his legs wouldn't carry him away from Kaylee, his knees and hands would. Sweat poured off him, wetting both his body and hair, blocking his vision which had already started to change to that of the beast. He no longer saw in color, but the muted black and white common to his animal form, and yet, he still crawled, moving further away from Kaylee.

Lucas knew he was going to lose this battle of wills. He was going to change, wasn't a single doubt in his mind. As his bones started to break and reform, he called out in agony, hoping against hope the pack would come and stop him. The cries of pain turned into growls and howls, and he knew all was lost. He was too far into the shift to change back now; he had lost, and the beasts within had won.

Movement in front of him caught his eye before his mind was completely gone, and if he could have in this form, he would have smiled. Eric in his jet-black wolf form, Dylan in his deep gray with one white ear, and Macon with his speckled gray fur, stood at the end of the path, waiting for him to finish the change. The last thing he saw before the beast took over were the three wolves charging him. His last thought was he hoped he didn't harm them.

Lucas was coming back in phases, everything hurt. He knew he was moving, not on his own steam or that of the beast. The hard punch in his stomach made him realize someone was carrying him? His mind was fuzzy and disjointed, he couldn't wrap his head around anything. He heard people talking and tried to concentrate and realized it was Eric carrying him and he was talking to Danica. The words they were saying were garbled, but he still made them out.

"Go help Macon and Dylan, Lucas messed them up pretty bad. When you're done, come back here to help me with Lucas. Matt is trying to keep Marcus and Emily away long enough for us to clean up this damn mess."

"What happened?"

"I don't have time to tell you right now, Dani, just go help Macon and Dylan. I'm going to clean Lucas up the best I can, then you can take over. Go, now!"

He started to remember the fight. Eric had charged him head-on, the beast attacked, tearing at Eric with teeth and claws, taking him down quickly. Just when he was about to go for the kill, Dylan and Macon charged him from the side, moving him back from Eric. Lucas had fought harder, not wanting to give up his prey. Eric was the animal the beast wanted, it didn't consider Dylan or Macon anything more than an annoyance, obstacles to its prize.

Lucas threw Macon into a tree, grabbing the scruff around his neck, using his superior strength to hurl him. Hearing the yowl, the wolf made and the sound of bones breaking, appeased the beast, but only a little. It then went after Macon; his beast was larger than Dylan's, but slower. The beast seemed to know everything Lucas did, exactly how to attack each member of his pack for the best outcome.

The beast knew to stay on Macon's right side and attack his flank. Macon was a to the death fighter, it didn't matter if he were injured or not as long as he could move, he would fight. The beast knew this and took him down brutally, tearing at his legs and hindquarters. Driven by the yowls and hisses of pain, the beast continued its attack until Eric, once again, charged him.

That fight took longer, enraging the beast. Eric wasn't as predictable as the others, he fought with a strategy only he knew. It was one of the reasons the man was a Beta. His skills in battle were second to none. He and Lucas had sparred many times, and Eric always won, mainly because Lucas refused to use his Alpha or other attributes against him.

The beast planned on correcting that, it didn't like that Lucas had backed down to Eric in the past. He was Alpha, and Eric needed to know that. Lucas was jolted out of the memory when his body turned weightless, then landed on a hard surface. Eric was talking to him again; Lucas couldn't even open his eyes much less respond to the man, but what he was saying didn't make any sense.

"You fought hard my friend, you controlled the beast. We all know Marcus has been lying to us. Just rest and let us take care of you, everything will be okay, Alpha."

What the fuck? He hadn't controlled anything and why was Eric calling him Alpha? He wasn't the Alpha of anyone. He had failed, he hadn't stopped the shift, and he attacked his own pack with two things on his mind, blood and death.

Lucas' mind drifted back to the fight; whether it was from the pain or his mind was playing tricks on him, he saw the scene as if he was watching it from the sidelines. He could see Eric's wolf, bloody and hurt, but still fighting. Macon and Dylan were laying on the ground where the beast had left them to die. Matt was standing off to the side starting to strip off his clothes. Lucas felt fear at that moment, he didn't want Matt to join the fight, he didn't want to hurt him. He wanted to scream and rage to his brother to stay out of it.

Lucas groaned and tried to get away from the things he was seeing. He couldn't understand why he was even seeing it. He hadn't been an observer, none of this should be possible. A tinkling voice came into his head saying, Watch, Lucas, it isn't what you think, watch the beast.

That was when he saw himself for the first time in his Were/Vampire form, and he rebelled, thrashing on the bed, trying to dislodge the image. He hated the way he looked, what he'd tried to do, but he was frozen. He couldn't get away from it, couldn't get the scene of the fight out of his head, and the fucking little voice became more insistent. It demanded he watch, see himself and what he had done.

His beast was massive, four times his own body width and height. It was like his three forms combined to make this one. Lucas wanted to look away, he didn't want to see himself this way. He hadn't shifted into his usual wolf form, this was more like the nightmare version of Werewolves seen in movies or written about in books. He still had the form of a man, but everything was mixed and amplified.

The muscles on his body were huge, his tattoos were stretched and distorted under the dark gray fur. His normally long hair had grown longer and become more of a mane running down his back. His blue eyes were golden, so bright, they were more of a yellowish color and looked evil. His nose was that of the wolf, but shorter, more snubbed. His fangs were double their usual size, at least three inches long. His massive hands were tipped with razor sharp claws. He watched helplessly as Eric once again charged, and he used those claws to slice into his fur, throwing him away like a piece of garbage.

Lucas wanted to scream to the beast to stop, but all he could do was stare at the scene playing out before him. Matt charged next, Lucas tried to fight his frozen state, he needed to warn him, to stop him, but nothing happened. He couldn't do anything, but watch. Matt's wolf jumped and landed on the beast, attacking it, biting and clawing at it.

Lucas couldn't take anymore, he didn't want to see the beast hurt his brother. Screaming, he was finally able to dislodge the image of the fight from his head. Lucas was ashamed; he hadn't controlled himself, and he was hurting the people he cared about. Why hadn't they just brought a gun with a silver bullet in it and ended him? Lucas knew they had them. Hell, Marcus had threatened him with them enough. But the pack fought, and now, they were taking care of him. Eric had even called him Alpha.

Twisting his body, Lucas tried to force it to wake from this state. He needed to get away from the pack, but especially Kaylee. He would need to talk with Ruth. He would demand she remove him as Guardian, and he would run. Then everyone would be safe.

He felt a warm hand on his chest and knew Flynn was there, he could feel him calming him. He didn't want that, he didn't want to be calm right now. He wanted to wake the fuck up, so he could do what needed to be done. Still unable to move or even open his eyes, he heard Flynn talking to Eric, he assumed because shit, even his sense of smell, all his senses were failing him.

"He's fighting me, Eric, he doesn't want to be calmed, he wants to leave," Flynn said.

Fuck, Lucas felt bad, he could hear the sorrow in Flynn's voice. Marcus had done a number on this man. His purpose in the pack was to calm and no one was letting him do it, including Lucas. Thinking he wasn't any better than Marcus, he let the calm envelope him.

The feeling was unbelievable. Lucas' mind began to clear, but it brought on the pain. He felt the pressure of Flynn's hand leave him, but another softer hand replaced it. This hand was small, dainty even. His pain started to recede, and he knew Danica was healing him, caring for him. The warmth of her healing gifts encompassed his body.

He could feel the tears and abrasions to his skin start to stitch together and the bones which had been broken start to repair. It wasn't exactly a pleasant feeling, but it wasn't really a bad one, either. The calm Flynn had induced was helping to ease any discomfort he might have.

Lucas could already feel his vampire side healing his body, but it was slow, he was too weak from the blood loss. His Were side wasn't faring any better, there had been too much damage inflicted on his body.

Matt's frantic voice made Lucas fight through the calm and heat, so he could hear what his brother had to say.

"You need to hurry, Danica, Marcus and Emily will be here any second. If he finds you down here with Lucas, he'll punish you and the rest of us."

"I'm almost done, Matthias, he should rest more soundly now. I just need a couple more minutes, and he'll be fine. Marcus will never know about the fight."

"Dani, if he finds out about the attack in the woods, he'll put Lucas down. Luke can't protect himself now, and without him, I don't think any of us will be able to protect him from Marcus if he finds out."

"Lend me your strength then, so I can finish his healing. We can't have our Alpha vulnerable, now can we?" Danica said in her sweet, sing-song voice. Lucas had always liked her voice, it reminded him of bells chiming softly, but why was she also calling him Alpha, to Matt, no less. He expected his brother to balk or at least say something, but it didn't happen.

What shocked the shit out him even more was the warmth of Danica's healing increased a hundred-fold to the point he was burning up, but within seconds, all the pain was gone from his body. When he was able to open his eyes, it was to see Danica's form moving up the stairs and Matt standing at the bottom looking back at him.

"Sleep well, brother, all will be better in the morning. Your pack will protect you."

Chapter 10

Kaylee hadn't slept much that night, her mind plagued with why Lucas had run off so fast. She thought they had a connection. When she was finally able to get even a little sleep, she dreamed. She dreamed of things which scared her. It started out simple, her and Lucas talking. Him telling her about his family, and her telling him about hers. Then the dream became heated, and they were ripping each other's clothes off, just about to get to the good stuff when a man's voice interrupted them, and Lucas was gone.

Kaylee was in a place—dark, cold and barren. It was like being in a black hole of nothingness, except that damn voice. It offered her all kinds of things—money, power, and success. Kaylee hated the voice, hated the place, and just wanted the dream to go back to her and Lucas, but it was like she was caught in the nightmare and nothing could shake it. Over and over again, the voice would say All you have to do is come to me, Kaylee. It will all be yours if you come to me, accept me as your mate. Embrace the dark, repel the light, and you can have it all.

Kaylee forced herself from the sheets, not bothering to change out of her pajamas—yoga pants and a long-sleeved t-shirt—and went downstairs. She wanted a Diet Coke, and then, she wanted to track Lucas down to find out what happened yesterday. She needed him to tell her why he ran.

Her grandma was making breakfast, much the same as the day before, burning the hell out of it, but Kaylee didn't have the same warm and fuzzy thoughts this morning; her mind was unsettled. Going right for the refrigerator, she grabbed her Diet Coke and sat down at the table.

"Are you okay, Kaylee girl?" Grandma Ruth asked, looking very concerned. Kaylee hadn't gotten the chance to answer before her grandma was standing over her, placing her hand on her forehead, much like she'd done when Kaylee was a child, checking for a fever, then cupped Kaylee's cheek and shut her eyes.

"Why do you always do that? You check to see if I have a fever, then you cup my cheek and shut your eyes like you're looking for something in your mind," Kaylee asked.

"Oh, Kaylee, I'm not looking for anything, it's just a family tradition. I'm giving you a blessing of good health, that's all. Nothing for you to worry about," Grandma Ruth said as she moved away and took the seat across from her. Kaylee noticed she hadn't brought any of the food over to the table or even her coffee. She was just looking at her. "What's troubling you so, child?"

Kaylee knew her grandma meant well, but for some reason, she didn't want to tell her about Lucas or the dreams. She felt an intense need to keep both of those things to herself, so she answered the only way she could without completely lying to her grandma.

"Nothing Grandma, just a lot of stuff on my mind today. I think the move and the drive took more out of me than I thought. I just didn't sleep all that well last night."

"Oh, hon, you should have come down, I would have made you some tea. Being in a strange place always makes it difficult for me to sleep, and you've had so much change, no wonder you've had a problem sleeping deeply. Tonight, I'll make sure you have some of my special tea. You know how much it helped you in the past."

Yeah, she did, and Kaylee was starting to wonder about it. Kaylee had tried to buy some mint tea a few years back when she was having problems at work and the stress of trying to do everything on her own had caught up to her, but the name brand stuff with the bear on it saying "Sleepy Time" did nothing for her. Whereas, her grandma's tea put her to sleep, almost instantly. If she didn't know any better, she would think Grandma Ruth was slipping sleeping pills into it. But since the same result happened when she was still a child, she doubted it was true, at least, she hoped it wasn't. Didn't some overwhelmed parents give their kids Benadryl or cough syrup to knock their asses out or was that just a joke? She wouldn't put it past her grandma, but she wanted to believe she would never do that.

"Sounds great, Grandma. You know, you're going to have to give me the recipe for the tea someday. I tried to buy some in the supermarket, but it wasn't the same."

"Oh, child, it's a family recipe, I'll have to write it down for you. That stuff in the supermarkets is over-processed, it doesn't have the same effect as fresh mint and tea leaves. But don't you worry, while you're here, all you have to do is ask, and I'll whip you up a cup. Now, how about some breakfast?" Grandma Ruth asked, a smile on her face. Like what she said just made perfect sense, and Kaylee should accept it because it's just the way it was. For now, she would, but pretty soon she was going to get some answers. She wasn't the same naïve little girl, anymore and being at her grands for just one day was proving that. But Kaylee could only deal with one thing at a time, and right now, Lucas and his actions were her priority.

"Sorry, Grandma, but I'm just not hungry this morning. I think I'm going to go for a walk and let the fresh air clear my mind. Maybe if I walk long enough, I'll build up an appetite," Kaylee said. She doubted her words and from the look on her grandma's face, she did too.

"Okay, dear, whatever you think is best."

Kaylee hurried off to the trail leading to the cabin. Her grandpa hadn't been at breakfast, so she assumed he was working on the cabin, and if he was, Lucas would be there. Just like the day before, a weird, nervous feeling came over her, but she blew it off, thinking everyone had that feeling when walking alone in the woods or an isolated area, right?

Today though, it had a different feel to it than yesterday. The sun had been shining, but now it was hidden behind thick, dark, and gloomy clouds. Kaylee started to walk faster. She didn't like the look of the clouds and fog was starting to roll in out of nowhere. What the hell?

Kaylee's heart was beating so hard and fast, she was afraid the damn thing was going to come right out of her chest. She tried every excuse she could think of, talking to herself. This is perfectly normal, fog can happen at any time of the day, it's just nature at work. Yeah, that didn't help, and she didn't believe a word of it. I'm just freaked out because of the creepy dream. This is nothing. That didn't help either, so she started to jog; the faster she got to the cabin, the better she would feel.

Kaylee heard a branch crack and started running faster, only in a different direction. She knew someone was behind her, and she felt like she was being herded, like an animal. Looking back over her shoulder, but keeping her pace, she saw a figure of a man through the now incredibly thick fog, walking close behind her; it didn't feel right, he didn't feel right.

"You know, you shouldn't be out here by yourself," a voice said, scaring the hell out of her.

Kaylee stopped and spun around in a circle, looking for the person the voice belonged to, and faltered. She knew she should have kept running, but there was something familiar about the voice. Every little sound made her jump—the crunch of leaves, the call of a bird somewhere, and the heavy thud of boots hitting the earth.

"Who's there?" she asked, her voice cracking in fear.

The fog cleared a little, finally allowing her to see who the voice came from. Matt was leaning against a tree with his head down, the hood up on his sweatshirt.

"Who are you to tell me where I should and shouldn't be on my grandparent's property? Isn't it you who shouldn't be out here?" she said as snidely as possible, pissed off he would scare her like that.

Matt straightened his body from his leaning position, pushing the hood off his head, and looked at her.

"No, Kaylee, I'm supposed to be out here. It's you who shouldn't be out here alone, it's dangerous."

"Really," Kaylee snarked, her anger fueling her need to put this asshole in his place again. Kaylee stomped to where he stood and poked him in the chest. "Tell me why I'm in danger on this land, since you seem to know so much."

Matt didn't get a chance to answer her. Lucas came barreling at them from out of nowhere. When he got close to them, he addressed his brother first, ignoring Kaylee all together.

"Matthias, that's enough, leave her alone and go back to the house!!" Lucas yelled.

Kaylee's eyes were shooting back and forth between the brothers, like she was watching a tennis match. Lucas had a black eye and a bruise on his cheek. Matt wasn't looking much better with several smaller cuts and scrapes on his own face. What the hell had happened to them? Kaylee wondered. It wasn't the only thing she noticed. Now that she was actually looking closely at them, their eyes were different, just like the other day when Lucas took off running away from her. Lucas' normally blue eyes had a somewhat gold tone to them, now, the blue only showing around the edges. Matt's were the same, only his green showing around the edges, and both of their eyes were brighter, as if there was a light behind them or a glow.

Matt walked off mumbling, "My name is Matt stop calling me Matthias!" He hated the name, it's what Marcus called him when he was angry.

Lucas was watching him. Kaylee, on the other hand, was watching Lucas.

"Lucas. Your eyes changed colors!" Kaylee blurted out. At her statement, Lucas turned and looked at her, but his eyes were his usual blue again with none of the gold tones.

"You're seeing things, Kaylee," he dismissed.

Kaylee noticed it wasn't only his eyes which had changed, so had he. He wasn't smiling or warm like before, there was a coldness to him. She tried changing tactics; maybe if she got him to talk, she could figure out what the hell was going on.

"Lucas, why would your brother tell me I shouldn't be out here by myself?" Kaylee asked. When she tried to touch his arm, Lucas jumped away from her as if her touch was poison; after what they had shared yesterday that really hurt.

"Listen, Kaylee, you need to stay out of the woods unless one of your grands are with you. There are things out here which could hurt you. And you need to stay away from me and my brother," Lucas said, moving away from her.

Kaylee knew he was keeping something from her. He had a different look—worried or scared—on his face; it didn't make sense. She didn't know him that well, but she couldn't imagine much scared Lucas Valentin.

"Tell me what's going on, Lucas, and why you ran away yesterday?"

"Yesterday was nothing, Kaylee." Lucas put his hands up as if to ward her off. "You need to do what I said, stay out of the woods and away from me."

The words tore out a piece of her heart.

Chapter 11

The weeks went by in a blur for Kaylee since that day in the woods when Lucas demanded she stay away from him and his brother. She hadn't seen hide nor hair of him which hurt more than she cared to admit. Not even on her and Grandma's weekly trip to the store. Matt had apparently quit working there; Kaylee knew because she asked. She was desperate to get some answers why Lucas' attitude had changed so abruptly toward her. She had hoped Matt would be able to help her out, but like his brother, he seemed to have disappeared from the planet.

That wasn't exactly right because she knew Lucas had been around, she could feel him. A couple of nights before, when she went to bed, she had seen him standing by the shed, watching her. She never got the feeling he was watching her like a creepy, peeping Tom, more like he was watching over her to keep her safe from the dangers he had talked about. The one time she ran out to talk to him, he had already been gone before she made it out the door.

Other weird things were going on, too. Kaylee hadn't moved out to the cabin even though she knew it was ready because her grandpa had taken ill, staying in bed most of the time or at least that's what her Grandma Ruth said. Kaylee had only seen him a handful of times, and the truth was, he didn't look at all sick to her. She didn't want to believe her grands would lie to her in such a way, but things weren't adding up, only confusing her more.

Then there were the dreams and that damn tea. Every night, her Grandma Ruth would fix the drink for her, and Kaylee would gulp it down like a good little girl, even though she didn't want to. It didn't make sense; she would repeat time and time again to herself she wasn't going to drink the damn tea, but as soon as the cup was put in her hand or placed in front of her, she drank it. Then she would go to sleep, and the man's voice would be there.

Lucas' presence, however, was absent. She felt like he was trying to break through the black to get to her, but he never made it. The only thing she heard was the voice, offering her everything she had ever wanted—a great job, money, and even a damn cat. He would say she could have it all, she only had to come to him. Every night her answer was the same, NO. She started hating even the thought of going to bed at night.

Kaylee had started to spend as much time in her room as possible, avoiding her grands, but tonight was going to be different. She was going to sit her Grandma Ruth down and demand some answers. When she walked into the kitchen, she wasn't surprised her Grandma Ruth was sitting at the table waiting for her, but what did surprise her though was there wasn't a cup of tea on the table, only a book. Kaylee walked to the table and sat down, not saying a word.

"Kaylee, there are some things I need to talk to you about," she said, tapping her finger against the book. Kaylee looked down briefly and noticed the book was large, but it also looked incredibly old.

"Okay," she answered, looking back up at her grandma. Kaylee was done asking questions and not getting any answers. If her grandma was going to talk, Kaylee would listen. Then she would demand, not ask, what she wanted to know.

"Your birthday is next week, and I need to start preparing your Ostara ceremony."

"My what?" Kaylee looked at her grandma, thoroughly confused.

"Your Ostara, Kaylee." Grandma Ruth groused. "It's the day you will come into your powers."

"My what?" Kaylee asked, shocked at what she was hearing.

"Your magic, Kaylee. You come from a long line of witches. You, though, are different, you're to become a high priestess. You will gain knowledge of all your powers, along with all the family spells and potions. It will come to you at all once. You were born on the day of the blue moon, and your Ostara will fall on another. In our world it means your magic will be legendary. The strongest of your generation."

Kaylee laughed, she wasn't the strongest of anything.

"I knew keeping this from you and binding your magic was a bad idea, but your mother wanted you to have a normal life until there wasn't any choice. Well, there isn't any now. You will come into your powers on your twenty-fifth birthday. You will have two moon rises to decide whether that magic is used for the light or for the dark. Do you hear what I'm saying to you, Kaylee? This is nothing to laugh about!" her grandma shouted.

Kaylee's brain was having a hard time keeping up, but one thing her Grandma had said stood out against the rest, and the puzzle pieces of her life started to snap together.

"You bound me?" Getting up from the table Kaylee began to pace around the kitchen, every few seconds looking back at her grandma. "The voices, the colors I saw, feeling other people's feelings, and seeing the animals around people? That's what you bound me from." It wasn't a question, but a statement. Looking at her grandma, she knew it was all true. "The tea, the tea you're still giving me today and the blessing you said you were giving me, it wasn't any of that, was it?" Kaylee accused.

"Yes."

"How dare you!" Kaylee barked. "It's because of you and my mother that I've felt defective my entire life. Tell me, Grandmother, you took the colors, animals, and feelings away, but why not the voices? Leaving just a little to bury the knife in my back?" Kaylee wasn't anywhere close to being done. She walked back to the table placing her hands on it, so she was eye level once again with her grandma and questioned.

"Let's talk about my mother. Why isn't she here 'preparing' me? If she could force you to bind me, why isn't she here now or couldn't she be bothered?"

"She will be here for your Ostara ceremony, along with your father, aunts, uncles, and cousins. The McClane family must come together to welcome your magic. Otherwise, it will be tempted to go to the dark side. Kaylee, you need to tell me about the voices. I know you're mad right now, but it's important. Nothing should have been able to get through the spell I placed on the tea. You should not have seen or heard anything from the magic realm."

"Well, I hate to disappoint you, but your spell didn't work. Every night for the past three weeks, a voice consumes my sleeping hours, promising me things, wanting me to go him. I say no, but he still comes.

"Now, explain what you just said. What family? I don't have aunts, uncles, or cousins. The only family I have is you, Grandpa, Mom, and my father. Who are these people you're talking about?"

"Kaylee your mother decided with your magic being so powerful at a young age, it was too dangerous to allow anyone else to interact with you. Since we were binding you, and the others have never been bound, you would have seen and questioned things she didn't want to answer."

That sounded like her mother. The woman was selfish and a bitch. All this talk of magic made her remember something, so since her grandma was in such a talkative mood.

"What's up with Lucas and why do I get the feeling you and Grandpa want me to stay away from him?"

"Lucas is the McClane family Guardian. He is a Were, or he was at birth." Her Grandma Ruth sighed, being put out by answering this particular question. "He's now Were and Vampire mixed. Your grandpa and I feel a mating with you and Lucas wouldn't have good results. Had he not been turned by the Vampires while he was in New Orleans, we would not object to the mating or you being around him. We knew it was a risk bringing you here while he was close, but it was a risk we had to take.

"The powers you have attracted him even more. We knew this when you came to stay here although, the last three weeks, his avoidance of you has been completely his doing. I don't believe in messing with Fate, only nudging it a bit.

"Now, listen, Kaylee, we have more important things to discuss besides you and Lucas and what may or may not happen," Grandma said, tapping on the book. Kaylee thought what they were discussing already was pretty damn important, so she just raised her eyebrow and crossed her arms over her chest, standing there like a five-year-old not getting their way.

"This is the McClane family grimoire," Grandma Ruth said as if the statement was the most important one Kaylee would never hear. She even had a gleam in her eye and a smile on her face. Kaylee wasn't in the mood to smile back.

"A grim what?" Kaylee asked.

"Don't you watch television or read?" Grandma Ruth had lost her smile and the gleam in her eye was gone. "It's a grimoire, the book which holds all the family spells, potions, and rituals." When Kaylee didn't look impressed or question her, she barked, "Our family has possessed this since the fifteen hundreds. Many wise and noble witches have held it in their hands. Every witch who had the book in their possession has added to it year after year. Now it belongs to you, and you will do the same."

"Hold up! Did you say potion? As in hocus pocus? Where the hell is the black caldron then or my broom? Do I get one of those, too?" Kaylee asked sarcastically.

"Listen to me, little girl, this is serious, it's your future. Every page in this book is powerful and in the wrong hands, could be devastating. You're about to turn twenty-five. It's time to grow up and stop acting like a child."

"Fine, you're a witch, so am I, and I have a family I didn't even know about, and in a couple of days, we'll have a ceremony which will bring forth my magical abilities. Is there anything else? Oh, wait don't answer that because there already is. You lied to me, my own mother lied to me. I told you about the things I saw and heard, the things my magic brought me, and you said it was my imagination. You fed me tea and made me forget. If that wasn't enough, you decided there was something wrong with the attraction I felt toward Lucas, and you interfered again, all because of my supposed magic.

"I don't want to hear anything else." Kaylee got up and grabbed her coat. "Right now, I don't even want to look at you, and you better get on the phone or use your witchy powers, whichever works best, and tell my mother to stay the hell away, because I'll slap her if I see her anytime soon."

Kaylee didn't look back; she opened and slammed the door and ran. Ran for the one place she knew would allow her to wrap her head around all of what her grandma had just told her. The tears were streaming down her face, causing her steps to falter several times. They had lied to her, all of them.

Kaylee had never felt short of breath, but this time... this time she felt as if she'd been running for miles. She was so pissed, it was taking all she could do not to hyperventilate.

Magic powers, spells, potions, and becoming the strongest witch in the history of our family. But this wasn't anything out of the norm, according to Ruth. Once she got to the edge of the pathway, Kaylee decided to take the trail around the backside of the pond. When she was younger, she'd always loved sitting on the bench there to clear her thoughts and fish with her Grandad.

She slowed to a fast walk, and things started piling up in her mind. She hadn't had the tea the night before. She could hear things coming from all over the woods and weird noises coming from the pond. The trees looked much greener, the sky bluer, and it was like nature was once again speaking to her. She hadn't felt or seen things like this since she was a little girl. Had Ruth released her from the bind or were her powers this strong now because she didn't drink the tea? She'd never had these feelings before.

Her breath still labored, she sat still on the bench, listening to the sounds from the pond as if she could hear faint little voices speaking to her. Thoughts of what Lucas and Matt had told her about not being out here alone started to creep into the back of her mind, freaking her out a little; among those thoughts were Lucas being a werewolf-vampire or whatever the hell Ruth was babbling on about back at the cabin.

Kaylee was shaken out of her thoughts when she heard someone or something running toward her from behind. Who was there and what the fuck is going on in these woods?

Chapter 12

Lucas had been sticking close to home for days. He went out only when he sensed Kaylee. He would track her down and watch, staying out of sight, staying in the shadows, making sure she was okay and nothing touched her. Even being in the shadows, she still called to him; she called to him all the time. His animal and vampire were becoming harder and harder to control, but he was determined he would win this fight. He would keep Kaylee safe, even from him. Especially from him.

He hadn't shifted in weeks too afraid the beast would come back and go after Kaylee. The vampire side of him hungered like no other time in his life. He was going through bags of blood at an alarming rate, but it never once quenched his hunger. And Marcus was getting more violent and demanding.

Every time Lucas walked past or caught sight of one of his pack mates, it was like they were pleading with him to do something. Each of them had come to him, except for Matt and Emily, and pledged their allegiance if he decided to become Alpha. He appreciated the support, but didn't have the first clue what he was ultimately going to do. He needed to get himself under control before he took on the pack.

Deciding to take a run in human form to get away from everything for a little while, he took off running, no destination in mind. He didn't even stick to the trails. His mind was chaotic and so was his direction. He should have known even mindlessly running through the woods would lead him right to her.

Lucas could sense Kaylee was somewhere close by; her scent was unique and completely Kaylee, he would be able to find her anywhere. The scent and promise of just one glance at Kaylee made him turn and head toward her. He wasn't surprised when the pond came into view. This seemed to be her favorite place. She had spent days inside her grands house over the weeks, only coming out once in a while to come here or run errands with her Grandma Ruth.

Seeing her sitting on the bench, crying, was breaking his heart and his resolve. Every time he saw her, she had been so sad, and he knew some of it was his fault. Lucas had given her up, so she would be safe and happy, but she wasn't happy. As for being safe, he had controlled himself for the last few weeks. Maybe when Kaylee came into her powers, she could bind him and they could still be together.

Then he remembered the voice telling him to watch the fight. Before, he had been too angry at himself to look at it objectively, but now he realized one very important thing. There had been countless times he could have killed his pack mates, yet he didn't. The beasts didn't. They fought and even maimed, but they didn't kill. They could have at any time; Lucas knew in that form he was unstoppable. He wondered if, maybe, he had more control over them than he first thought.

Seeing her now, scared, tears staining her cheeks, he wanted to believe it was true. The little voice came again in his mind; this time it said, Go with your heart. Lucas shook his head, trying to rid himself of the voice, but it kept on repeating itself. Lucas couldn't take it anymore. He was going to do what the damn voice said and go with his heart, and his heart was consumed by Kaylee. Not wasting another second, he took off running toward her. Just as he got within a foot of her, he stopped, smiling like a fool.

"Damn it, Lucas, you scared the shit out of me!" Kaylee yelled, standing, slapping him on his chest, making him laugh, which of course pissed her off. His mate was a violent little thing; Lucas loved it.

"Why are you laughing?" Kaylee screeched. "You've been avoiding me for weeks since your little declaration in the woods, and now, you come running out of the same damn woods like the hounds of hell are on your heels, only to laugh me? What is wrong with you?"

"Kaylee, I'm sorry," Lucas said tentatively, putting his hands on her shoulders to see if she would accept his touch. When she didn't fight it, he pulled her close, hugging her to his body. "Why are you out here all alone, Kaylee? It's not safe." Kaylee pulled, but Lucas wasn't going to let her go; he had her in his arms and planned to keep her there.

"I'm so sick of all of you telling me what's good for me. Telling me things which shouldn't be possible. I needed a break, so I took it," Kaylee said, her eyes glistening with tears.

Lucas pulled her back into his chest and this time she burrowed deeper. He was sure if it was possible, she would have buried herself right into his skin.

"Tell me, babe, let me help you with this. I promise not to run like the last time. I'll even promise to explain it all to you, but one problem at a time, okay?" Lucas said, rubbing her back.

"It's nothing and everything," Kaylee sniffled. "You, my grandparents, my freaking life. Oh, and let's not forget my destiny. Oh no, we can't forget that, now can we because, apparently, I'm the only one who didn't know about it? Is that enough for you?"

This time when she pulled back, Lucas let her. She needed to get all of this out, and he didn't blame her for using him as her personal punching bag. He deserved it for the way he had dismissed her and what they could have.

"That's not all of it, is it babe?" Lucas questioned, knowing it wasn't. Kaylee completely left the circle of his arms, and he felt the loss to his soul.

"What the hell is with all the babe stuff, Lucas? Why now? Just a few weeks ago it was nothing, I was nothing, or at least that's how you made me feel. Now it's babe this and babe that, where do you get off?"

"Kaylee, listen, I know I need to explain myself and my actions, but could we maybe go into the cabin and talk about it. I don't like you being out here, so exposed to everything."

"No, you tell me what you have to say, then leave. This time it's going to be my choice, Lucas. Your actions hurt me, and I'm sick of everyone I care about hurting me. It's time to make some changes and stop being the doormat I've been for the last twenty-five years."

"Kaylee, you're not a doormat. Hell, I never once thought that. I'm so sorry I hurt you, but after that kiss, shit. I didn't run from you to avoid being with you, I ran to avoid hurting you. I was born a Were, and my animal is a wolf. I am also Vampire, which makes me a Were/Vampire hybrid. I had to run, Kaylee, my Vampire tasted your blood and my wolf wanted to mate.

"The two fought to get out, and I started to shift. I didn't know what my beast would do, and I feared it would hurt you, so I ran. My job is to protect you, even from me, can you understand that? Plus, hell, I didn't want you to see me like that. It's also against the rules until your Ostara has taken place. You are still very much human, and if you saw my beast, I would be thrown from my pack or worse."

"Yeah, well, Grandmother seems to like to tell everyone's secrets, so I already knew. Besides, I knew there was something different about you before she confirmed it. On the very first night I was here, I somehow knew you were different, Lucas, that you would mean more to me, and then that day at the pond, I saw you shift at the edge of the woods. Unfortunately, because of my grandmother's special tea, I had forgotten all about it until I stopped drinking it, but it's all coming back to me. Your fine ass running for the woods should have stuck with me, but my grandmother's tea is potent. The only thing it can't seem to do it get rid of the damn voices."

"What voices, Kaylee?" Lucas grabbed her shoulders again, so she would focus completely on him. "This is really important. Do you know who they came from, do you recognize the voice, and when do you hear them? Is it only when you're sleeping, or is it all the time?"

"At night, when I'm sleeping," Kaylee pulled away again and started walking, "but in the last few days, it happens any time, and no, I have no clue who it is. The only thing I can give you is it's a guy, and he creeps me out. Still think I'm just an ordinary human?"

Lucas followed Kaylee. It seemed she was in the mood for a power walk because even though his legs and stride were longer than hers, she was moving fast.

"Kaylee, listen, I know this is a lot to take in, but I promise, I will help you get through it."

"Really, Lucas, you're going to help me get through it when you just dumped me like trash not that long ago? I'm just supposed to believe you, right now, because you said so? Well, let me clue you in. I don't have time to let you help me. In a few days, I have to decide if I want to be a good witch or a bad one. What are your thoughts on that?"

"My thoughts are you will choose the side of the light because it's in your very nature to do so."

"And you know this, how?"

"Because I know you, I feel you, Kaylee," Lucas grabbed her elbow and spun her around, slapping his hand against his chest, "in here. Do you understand what I'm saying? I feel you in my heart, have since the moment we met, and there isn't anything evil about you."

"Is that you talking, Lucas, or the Guardian of the McClane witches?" Kaylee asked, yanking her arm out of his hold, turning away from him, once again walking away. Lucas was getting pretty sick of her walking away from him all the time.

"Yes, Kaylee, I am the Guardian of the McClane witches, but I am also a man. I am here to protect the McClane family at all costs that is my duty. I have no duty whatsoever to lie to you, and I promise I'll never do it again. I already explained why I had to run from you; I didn't want to hurt you, or more to the point, I feared hurting you." Lucas knew Kaylee was going to say something mean, just to hurt him, so he countered her before she got the chance.

"You have no idea how powerful you are, Kaylee. One taste of your blood brought me to my knees, literally. Your lineage and day of birth bring a hefty burden; for that, I'm sorry, but I know you'll prevail."

"How can you know that, Lucas? I don't even know that. I've been lied to so much, I don't know what's true anymore. How can I believe and trust you when the people who were supposed to have my back at all costs, lied to me over and over again? I don't even know why I'm so freaking special."

"Kaylee, one of my duties as Guardian is to keep the McClane family tree. I can tell you that you come from two of the strongest magical bloodlines in the world today. When your parents, Rebecca McClane and James Smith, joined, it sealed your fate. Being born on the blue moon cemented it. Your powers will be immense; they already are, and you haven't come into them fully.

"You need to listen to everything your Grandmother has to tell you. If you don't, it will be very dangerous for you and those around you. Just like my animal/vampire, you could have more power than you can control on your own. You'll need their help, just like I need my pack."

"It's just too much, Lucas. I need to forget about it for a little while. My mind is spinning and out of control with all the what ifs and only ifs. I need a break from all of it. Can you understand that?"

"Yeah, babe, I get it more than you know."

Chapter 13

Kaylee was conflicted. She wanted to forgive Lucas for running from her, especially now that she knew why he'd done it, but there was another part of her not exactly ready to forgive and forget, just yet. He had done what her mother and grandmother had been doing to her all her life, making decisions on her behalf without thinking about how Kaylee might feel about them.

Kaylee knew, deep down, she liked Lucas, hell, she more than liked him and wanted more; that's why him dismissing her had hurt so bad. He should have talked to her, but then again, he was talking to her now. He hadn't known Ruth had told her about him, and he gave her the information all on his own. Took him a while, but he'd still done it. Shouldn't that count for something?

Damn it, she'd just told him she didn't want to think and here she was thinking again, making her brain hurt. Maybe she should just go with her first instinct and let him help her forget for a while. Kaylee could think of one way to make that happen, and it wasn't playing monopoly. First though, she needed to see if he would continue to be honest with her, so she asked him two of the questions weighing on her mind.

"Lucas, did my grandparents warn you off from getting close to me?" Kaylee asked, stopping to look at him. She needed to see his face when he gave her his answer to that question because the next one was a doozy.

"Yes," Lucas sighed, rubbing his hand down his face, "but that didn't have anything to do with the decision I made to stay away from you. Edwin and Ruth want to protect you." When Kaylee started to say something, he held up his hand and stopped her. "No, please, listen. I didn't say it was right, or that they approached any of this in the right way, but they have their reasons. Reasons you need to talk to them about. But know this, Kaylee, it was my fear of hurting you which kept me away, nothing else. There isn't anything anyone could say to me which would have kept me away."

"But you still stayed away, you never talked to me about any of this. I get there were things you felt you couldn't say. Hell, I should have been scared from the first moment I realized you were Other, but I wasn't. I know it doesn't make sense, but you have to understand, if we're going to move forward, you can never do that again. You hurt me more by your actions than you could have ever done by your hands, claws, teeth, or fists. Because know this, Lucas Valentin, as much as you know in your heart I will choose the side of light, I know you nor your beasts would ever hurt me. You're not capable of it, even in full shifted form."

"Kaylee, you can't know that for sure. Hell, I don't even know that for sure, and it scares the fuck out of me," Lucas said, gritting his teeth. "When you come into your magic, I think you should bind me, keep those sides of me from merging. It's the only way I'll know for sure you'll be safe."

"But that's just it, Lucas, I wouldn't be safe if you couldn't protect me and do your job as Guardian. You need to trust me, and most importantly, trust yourself. I know a way you can be sure of that without any additional magic. Are you willing to try?"

Lucas groaned and started to walk away only to turn swiftly and come right back to where Kaylee was standing.

"I know what you're going to ask me to do, Kaylee, and it's too dangerous. You wouldn't be protected; there's more I haven't told you. I am drawn to you, so are my vampire and wolf because you are my mate."

"Mate?"

"Yes, mate. The one person in this world who is meant for me, the only person who can complete me. If we go further, if we fuck, then I'll want to claim you by marking you, biting you, so both the animal and vampire within me bond to you. It means taking your blood and risking what happened before. I can't do it unless you're protected."

"So, basically, what you're telling me is we're fated in some way? I don't really get this whole mate thing. Is it like marriage? And it can only happen when you bite me and drink my blood?"

"Yes and no. Mating bonds the souls, so it's more than a human marriage. It's also for life, there's no divorce, ever. If one of us dies, the other will follow. You're still very much human, Kaylee. I can't ask you to make that decision. I'm already connected to you, I already have feelings for you, but until you come into your magic, you won't fully understand what's going on."

"Let's get something straight, right now, okay?" Kaylee laughed, sarcastically. "You're not in my mind, you don't know my feelings, but I'm drawn to you like no other man." At the mention of other men, Lucas growled low and deep, but Kaylee ignored him, she had other things she wanted to say. "I have strong feelings for you, otherwise, I wouldn't have been so badly hurt by your actions and rejection. I'm trusting you to never do that again."

"Kaylee," Lucas implored. She knew he was going to give her the same reasoning again, and she didn't want to hear it.

"No, this isn't something you get to decide for both of us. I want you, my panties have been wet since the moment I met you. I don't know if it's because of something fate has decided or because you are sexy as hell. I want to believe what you're telling me. I want a future with you, but to have it, you have to trust me and yourself. Shift, Lucas, prove to both of us you won't hurt me, and we can have that future."

Kaylee watched as Lucas paced back and forth in front of her, running his hands through his beautiful dark hair. She wanted to be the one who was doing that, but until he agreed and proved to himself his Other side would always keep her safe, that couldn't happen because there would always be something between them. Kaylee wanted to mate with Lucas, it was instinctual and explained so much about how she'd been feeling. She watched as Lucas finally made a decision and started to take off his clothes.

"If we're going to do this, you need to stand back, and you need to take this. Lucas handed her a heavy object wrapped in thick leather. Kaylee started to open the leather and when she saw the gun, she almost dropped it. Lucas was there instantly steadying her hand.

"Why?"

"Kaylee, listen, this is the only way I'll do this, you need to be protected. If what comes out of my body isn't just my wolf, you need to use that," Lucas said pointing at the gun. "It's loaded with silver bullets, one of the things humans got right in folklore. It will put the beast down; the silver will stop it."

"I can't shoot you, Lucas!" Kaylee screamed.

"You can and you will or all of this stops now. Did Edwin teach you how to shoot? Do you know how to use the gun, or do you need me to show you?"

With shaking hands, Kaylee tried to get some of the moisture back into her mouth, so she could answer him, but her mind was again plagued with questions. How could he ask her to do this? She had just told him she wanted a future, and he was telling her to end it before it even got started.

She managed a whispered, "I know how to use it," but then needed to turn away for a second. Kaylee realized she needed to be as strong as Lucas. He was going to do something he feared because she asked him to. She needed to trust what she believed was true, really was; he wouldn't hurt her, so the gun wouldn't be needed at all.

"Okay," Kaylee said, clicking off the gun safety. "I promise if at any point your beast goes to attack me, I will shoot. That's all I can promise, Lucas. Regardless of what comes out of your body, I will not shoot unless it is absolutely necessary."

This time when he started to take off his clothes, Kaylee was too preoccupied by the gun in her hand to truly appreciate his beauty. His shirt already gone, he kicked off his heavy boots, bending to remove his pants. She wasn't the least bit ashamed to admit that even in her state of fear, she glanced at his lower region to get a peek at his manhood. Unfortunately, she missed it because he never straightened his body. There was a blur or glimmer, she wasn't sure which, and a coal black wolf was standing in front of her, instead of Lucas. This wolf was bigger than any wolf she had ever seen in the wild or captivity. His eyes were the most amazing shade of copper. She didn't feel one iota of fear.

Dropping the gun and falling to her knees, Kaylee held her hands out to the wolf and waited. The wolf was cautious, but within seconds, he came to her. Kaylee let him smell her, laughing at how his cold nose felt against her hand. Feeling braver, Kaylee moved her hand to the scruff of the wolf's neck, running her fingers through the thick fur. When the wolf moved closer and licked her cheek, Kaylee giggled and knew in her heart, she would never have anything to fear from Lucas or his Other side.

Then they played; it was just what Kaylee needed. She ran around, laughing, letting the wolf chase her. The wolf got in her way, causing her to fall to the ground, but she noticed he took most of her weight and prevented her from any harm. Kaylee was laying on her back looking up at the wolf, laughing. She started to pet him again, and he nuzzled her with his snout, making her laugh harder. This was the happiest she had felt in a really long time.

Kaylee was so overjoyed, she hugged the animal close. One minute she was hugging fur and fighting off wolf licks, the next, she was hugging warm skin. Kaylee pulled back a little and smiled.

"Your animal is beautiful, and Lucas, I was right, you could never hurt me." And then he was kissing her, all six-foot-four naked inch of him.

Chapter 14

Kaylee was in heaven! She loved the feeling of Lucas' weight on top of her body. The feel of his hard length pressed against her most intimate spot made her core soften and weep, preparing her for his possession. The merriment she had felt playing with his wolf left her, and a new feeling enveloped her body—need, lust, and heat were controlling her actions now. Kaylee boldly leaned forward and kissed him deeply.

"I told you, Lucas, you'll never hurt me, no part of you could ever hurt me," she said, cupping his face, pulling him back to her.

This time though, Kaylee wasn't the aggressor with the kiss as she intended. Lucas was in full control, taking the kiss from sweet and sultry to hot and urgent at Mach speed. Kaylee wasn't passive though, she was just as needy for him as he seemed to be for her. Lucas used every part of him in the kiss. His tongue penetrated her mouth with force, thrusting in a way which promised more. His lips devoured hers, only to stop, so he could place tiny little nips against her own when she tried to take over, showing her who was in charge.

Kaylee couldn't think of a single place she would rather be. She loved the way Lucas was playing her body like the strings on a guitar, like the rock star she thought he was the day they met. The way he laid his tall, lanky body, caging her from head to toe, caused spirals of delight to course throughout her. Kaylee wasn't going to miss this opportunity to finally touch him, all of him. Using her hands, she explored every inch of his smooth skin within reach. Rubbing his sides, shoulders, and back, longing to be able to feel more.

She knew he approved by the sounds he was making and the urgency of his own movements as he kissed her deeper. When he dropped his hips and ground against her, she knew by the long, thick, hard length of him, he was just as aroused as she was. His hands were sliding over her clothes, making her wish for the power to make them disappear, so she was just as naked as he was. Kaylee moved her hands lower, cupping his ass to bring him more firmly against where she needed him most.

Lucas stopped her, pulling her hands back, then linking them together with his, lifting them until he held them over her head. Kaylee grunted her disapproval while nipping his supple bottom lip with her teeth. Lucas smiled against her lips, then pulled her arms up further, causing her breasts to rub up against his muscular chest. Kaylee couldn't help her throaty moan. The sensation of the fabric covering her breast abrading her skin in just the right way caused her nipples to tighten even further. Wanting more, Kaylee arched her back, pushing herself even further into him. Lucas started kissing his way down her neck; Kaylee almost wanted to cry when he stopped to take her in.

"Damn, Kaylee, you smell so good, I can't get enough of you," Lucas said as he once again pressed into her body. When he suddenly stood, Kaylee was going to protest, but the sight of him in all his naked glory stopped her. This man was gorgeous. The sight of him simply took her breath away.

He was so cut and perfect, he seemed unreal to her; the fact he wanted her only increased her desire for him. She was a simple girl; she knew she was cute, not necessarily pretty, but cute, at least, that's what everyone had always said. Having this gorgeous man look at her the way he did made her feel beautiful for the first time in her life.

She wasn't in his league, not even close, but damn, she was going to go for it with everything she had. He didn't have a single flaw, from his beautiful face to his sculpted chest, she let her eyes travel down to his amazing eight-pack. Leaning against that eight-pack was the largest cock she had ever seen; it was so long it stretched above his navel and was thick enough, she was sure her fingers wouldn't be able to meet when she put them around the beast. Something she wanted to do, but refrained because she wanted to see what he planned next. If he stopped this, she would take matters, literally, into her own hands and change his mind.

She couldn't stop herself from licking her lips though. Lucas must have liked that because his cock twitched and a bead of pearly white pre-cum dotted the angry, red head of his plum-shaped crown. Kaylee wanted to taste him, lick him like an ice cream cone, leaving no vein, notch, or silky piece of skin unmarked by her touch. She wanted to feel that thickness in her mouth as it stretched her lips and jaw. The ache in her center increased, causing her to rub her thighs together, adding some friction, trying to relieve the ache on her own.

Their make-out session, plus the sight of him, and she was on the verge of coming. All she needed was just a little more pressure, and she would explode in a million little pieces. Lucas' growl should have stopped her, but she was too far gone, she needed more, she needed him.

"Kaylee, I want to be a gentleman, but if you keep looking at me like that, all bets are off. I'm going to fuck you right here on the cold ground and not give one fuck about who might see us or hear you scream." Kaylee wanted to plead with him, hell, beg him to make that happen. "You deserve better than that. I want to spend hours touching, tasting, and taking your body, that can't happen out here."

Kaylee didn't care about what Lucas thought she deserved, she only knew that, at that moment, she wanted him desperately. Lucas made the decision for her, grabbing her hand and pulling her to her feet. The move took Kaylee by surprise, caused her balance to falter, and her to fall into his body. The feel of his warm skin under her palms made them both moan in pleasure. Her hands planted on his chest, on impulse, she brushed her thumbs across his nipples.

"Fuck it," Lucas said and scooped her up, throwing Kaylee over his shoulder. "Time for you to meet my vampire side, babe, hold on."

Kaylee gasped at the impact of her stomach hitting his shoulder, but his urgency added to the Neanderthal move turned her on even more. She should have been paying attention to what Lucas had said instead of what her body demanded because when he took off, the landscape blurred, it was dizzying. She felt the solidness of his shoulder, but the rest of her felt weightless, like she was flying. His speed truly amazed her.

One minute they were moving, and the next, they had stopped. She could hear Lucas' feet pounding up the stairs, and when she pulled her body up, using his ass as a brace, she realized they were at her cabin. Lucas didn't put her down until they were through the door.

Once her feet hit the solid surface, he had her pushed up against the wall next to the door. Lucas placed open-mouth kisses to her jaw and throat, sucking lightly with each kiss, only to come back to her mouth, devouring her again.

Desperate to feel her skin against his, Kaylee started to take off her clothes while Lucas showered her with his amazing kisses. Her jacket was easy; already left open, she just nudged it off her shoulders and it fell to the ground. Kaylee didn't want to interrupt the delicious things Lucas was doing to her neck, but she needed her shirt and bra gone.

Lucas solved the problem for her by ripping the fabric of her t-shirt down the middle, exposing her black lace-covered breasts. Kaylee arched into him, rubbing the rough fabric over her distended nipples. She had never in her life been so thankful for choosing this specific bra. Lucas moved his hand between them, using his adept fingers to snap open her bra with a flick of his fingers, allowing her heavy breast to spill free, landing freely in his open palm. He continued kissing her neck and shoulder, moving his lips closer with each one of her panted breaths to the prize he held in his hands. The moment his lips made contact with her breast, Kaylee screamed out his name.

Lucas didn't stop, continuing to play her like a well-used guitar, strumming, plucking, and gliding his mouth and fingers across her breasts, mumbling "Damn, Kaylee" every time she moaned or moved closer to her release.

After a while, the pleasure became too much. Kaylee let out a deep gasp and tried to push him away, but Lucas grabbed her chin, making her look deep into his beautiful, gold eyes. She knew both his Beasts were close, making the moment more special. She wanted all of him.

"Kaylee, I want you, tell me you want me back, otherwise this all stops now," Lucas growled in an inhuman voice.

"Yes, Lucas, take me, please, I can't handle much more."

Lucas smiled at her, brushing his fingertip against her cheek, slowly moving it down to her throat. After a few brushes of his fingers, he encircled her neck with his hand, applying a little pressure, not enough to hurt her or make it difficult to breathe, just enough to let her know he was in control, and they would be doing things his way. It was the first time she saw his dominate nature, and it only added to all that she was feeling.

"You're mine, Kaylee, I can't fully claim you yet, not until you've come into your magic, but by saying yes, know that one day soon, I will be making that claim and everyone will know exactly who you belong to, understand?"

Kaylee moaned, she wanted that and so much more, "Yes, Lucas, please, just do something," Kaylee begged. "I've never felt like this before, it's almost too much."

"It will never be too much between us, Kaylee, it will always be everything."

She felt his other hand brush over the waistband of her jeans. When he moved his hand off of her neck, she mourned its loss. She liked the feeling of safety and control it provided because, right now, everything was out of control. She had never been aroused to the point of pain, but that's where she found herself now, and Lucas was the only thing holding her together.

Lucas brushed his hand down the side of her neck to her chest, stroking lightly across the side of her breast down to her to hip. Her skin was so sensitized, she started to tremble.

When he got down on his knees, she sucked in a breath; Kaylee doubted this man ever got on his knees for any reason. He was too strong, too dominant to kneel before anyone; that he was doing it before her, in Kaylee's mind, further cemented his feelings for her. As he started kissing a line down her body, Kaylee fell back against the wall. Her legs were shaking so badly, she had to lock them to remain standing. When he circled her bellybutton with his tongue, Kaylee's core clenched, releasing more of her arousal into her already soaked panties.

Panties which, a second later, lay on the floor, somewhere behind him. How he had managed to strip her of her pants and underwear without her knowledge was beyond her comprehension at the moment, she was just so happy they were gone from her body. When his nose nuzzled her mound, she could feel herself blossoming for him.

"I need to taste you Kaylee. Your scent, the smell of honeysuckle, has been driving me crazy since the first day we met."

"Please, Lucas, anything." She felt his tongue as it penetrated her slit, licking through her folds until he flattened it against her clit. Kaylee had a fleeting thought—the kisses he had given her before were amazing, but this one was by far her favorite. It only took seconds for her to explode, her body slumping in ecstasy.

Lucas only allowed her a second to catch her breath and come back to earth. He grabbed her ass, lifting her up. Kaylee instinctively wrapped her legs around his waist, her arms around his shoulders.

"Babe, this is going to be quick. I need you so much, I don't know how long I'm going to last without feeling your heat around my cock."

"Please, I need that too, hurry," Kaylee pleaded, tilting her hips forward. The move brought his cock to the opening of her slick channel. Kaylee knew if she moved her hips just a little, he would be inside her, exactly where she wanted him, but Lucas had other ideas.

He stopped her movements with a firmer grip on her ass and hips and asked, "Are you sure you want this Kaylee? Are you sure you want me to make you mine?"

"YES!!" Kaylee screamed. "Please, Lucas."

Her scream was all it took for Lucas to thrust into her body, not stopping until he was touching her womb, and they were joined together as one for the first time.

"Fuck, babe, you are so damn hot and tight," he said through gritted teeth.

Kaylee whimpered and tried to grind into him further, the ache in her belly had returning tenfold.

"Don't fucking move, Kaylee, or I'm going to lose it before this even begins, and I don't think either one of us wants that to happen. Just give me a minute to get myself under control. I want to hear all those dirty little noises you're making right now for the rest of the night, not just a few seconds."

Kaylee was already squirming and moaning uncontrollably, but she tried to do as he asked. The feel of him inside her body, stretching her so tight, felt amazing. But when he started to move, rocking back and forth, in and out, hitting all those spots in her, she couldn't hold back any longer, meeting him thrust for thrust. Urging him to go harder, faster.

"FUCK, YES, oh my God, Lucas," were the only coherent words Kaylee seemed capable of saying, and she repeated them all over and over.

"Cum, Kaylee, now!" Lucas barked. Kaylee's body responded as if it knew the truth of exactly who owned her; Lucas Valentin owned every inch of her. Seconds later, Kaylee blacked out as the most amazing orgasm exploded within her body. She saw fireworks, the stars, even the heavens. Sex had never been like this for her before, but then again, she was pretty sure her ecstasy had everything to do with this man and her feelings for him.

His thrust and retreats were coming faster now, harder, but with less rhythm; Kaylee knew he was going to come. She could feel him growing larger, stretching her further. Forcing her eyes open, she watched as he tilted his head back, neck muscles straining, veins popping, and yelled out her name. When she felt the molten hot splash of his cum hitting her womb, she went flying again. Only this time, she didn't come back from the flight.

Chapter 15

It took Lucas several minutes to be able to stand up straight or even consider walking. He'd known being with Kaylee was going to be an amazing experience, but he had never expected to be completely blown away. He had never come so hard in his life.

She had been so tight and wet for him, he had almost come way too soon. It had been a test of will over his body's needs and what his brain wanted. He was thankful his need to make her come while deep inside her won out; her pleasure would always come first.

Gripping her ass more firmly, Lucas stood, still deep within her and could feel his cock hardening again. Looking down at the bundle in his arms, he realized Kaylee was passed out cold; he smiled, kissing her forehead.

"Babe, are you okay?" When she didn't answer him, Lucas decided he needed to move this party to somewhere softer. He had plans for Kaylee.

Looking over his shoulder, he considered taking her upstairs to the king-sized bed he knew was up there, but his legs weren't quite ready to take the stairs. Spying the plush carpet in front of the stone fireplace, he decided it was the next best option. Turning with her still in his arms and himself lodge deeply, he groaned when the move caused his cock to lose its silken glove.

He would be inside her again soon enough, now, he needed to take care of her. Laying her out on the carpet, Lucas stood there for a few minutes, just looking at her. Kaylee was a goddess to him. Her long blond, purple-tipped hair spread around her like a halo. Her gorgeous face looked peaceful in her slumber, but the tinge of pink on her cheeks and the tiny smile on her lips made him think of a siren.

Seeing her shiver, Lucas jumped into action, grabbing the afghan and a couple of pillows off the couch. When he came back to his sleeping beauty, she had moved onto her side, curling up like a little cat. Getting on his knees, he brushed her hair from her face, gently lifting her head, placing the pillow beneath it. Just as he was about to cover her, he noticed his cum dripping from her, and a primal growl escaped his throat.

He should have felt shame; they had never discussed not using some type of protection, but the primal part of him liked smelling his scent mixed with Kaylee's. She'd been marked, no other Were would touch her with his scent within her body.

He knew there wasn't a chance of getting or receiving an STD because of his Were side. They were incapable of carrying or transmitting human disease. Even if by some chance he did contract something, his vampire side would heal it instantly. He knew she wouldn't become pregnant this time because it wasn't the right time for her body to conceive.

He almost groaned at the thought of her being in heat. Her scent would sharpen, become deeper, even more inviting, making his animal go crazy with lust and the need to plant his seed inside her. Lucas laid down, spooning her from behind. Brushing his fingers down her side, he rested his hand on her stomach and imagined the day she would be swollen with his child.

He had never once, in all of his twenty-seven years, considered having children. His duties to the McClane's and the discord which had plagued his pack weren't ideal for raising a family or hell, even thinking about the future. But this was Kaylee, she was everything. He wanted things with her he never imagined wanting, including children one day. They would need to discuss it, this was all too new to even consider it now, but one day, he hoped it would happen.

Replaying their love-making in his mind, Lucas almost cringed at how roughly he'd taken her. He had barely managed to control himself long enough to get her off and remembered how hard he'd had to fight his vampire half. The urge to bite her had overwhelmed him from the first kiss to the last. Lucas was still hesitant to let that happen. Kaylee said she trusted him, but he was still a long way from trusting himself enough to take her blood.

Lucas knew he would have to work on that, trusting himself, because their very future depended on it. Neither side of him could fully claim her without a bite and the exchange of blood. It was part of the mating ritual. However, those were thoughts for another time.

Lucas kissed her head and pulled her even closer, finally pulling the afghan over her body. He didn't need it, his Were side always kept him warm, but he wanted her protected from the cool cabin air. Lucas sent his senses out before shutting his eyes. He needed to make sure Kaylee was safe as they slumbered. Not sensing anything, but a couple of deer in the area, he finally let his eyes drift shut. With Kaylee in his arms and thoughts of the future on his mind, he realized he had never felt so content. Kaylee was his home.

Lucas and Kaylee spent three days huddled down in the cabin, learning everything there was to learn about each other. They talked, played, and fucked, constantly. He had known he wanted her, lusted after her, but the more he learned about Kaylee, the more he liked her as a person.

She was sweet and caring, and her family meant the world to her, even though she was mad at them right now. Lucas tried to help her understand the way of the Others in this new magical world she found herself in. He answered as many questions as he could, but told her only talking to Ruth would calm the turmoil in her mind.

Something else that concerned Lucas was neither the pack nor the McClanes had come near the cabin. He had sensed the pack nearby, but they never crossed the borders of the land. Last night, he sensed Edwin, but was thankful he'd stayed just outside the marked lands. Their mating was going to be hard for the pack to accept, but with what Edwin and even Ruth had said to him, he knew they would be their biggest problem. He just hoped the bond he and Kaylee were forming would be strong enough for her to choose him. He hated putting her in that position, but there wasn't a part of him which would let her go now. He had tried and failed.

Lucas felt Kaylee's fingers brush his face. When he looked down at her, she smiled. She had the freshly fucked look on her face—pink tinged cheeks, wild hair, and bright, half-laden eyes.

"What are you thinking about?" she asked.

"Nothing, everything, I'm just thinking, babe, go to sleep."

"Oh no, you don't. We agreed to do all of this together. Tell me what's on your mind, and we can figure out what to do about it," Kaylee said, lifting up from his chest, propping her head on her hand, giving him that look. The one every guy knows shows the woman they love means business. Lucas laughed and ran his finger down her wrinkled brow.

"It's just that the pack and your grandparents haven't come to check up on either of us. It doesn't make sense, we've been here for three days. Marcus alone should be rip-roaring mad I haven't been under this thumb. Then there are your grandparents; they don't agree with us being together, but I know deep down they love you. It just seems odd they haven't even tried to check up on you, you know what I mean?"

"Yeah, I was wondering that myself, but I'm not going to complain, we needed this time to get to know each other. Do you think your pack will give us problems? I'm not as worried about my grands, they love me. I know after I talk with them, they might not be happy, but they'll support me and my decision."

"Kaylee, I don't know if that's exactly true. I'm not an ideal mate for anyone because of my Vampire side, but your being the Blue Moon Priestess makes it an even bigger problem. The Coven could ban you, and you need them. After the ceremony, your powers will open, flow through you, but you haven't been prepared or trained. It could be overwhelming. When I woke up after being bitten, hell, babe, the combination of the Were and the Vampire was too much. It took me years to get it under control. I did horrible things. I don't want that for you."

Kaylee laid her head back down on Lucas' chest, rubbing her hand up and down. Lucas knew she was trying to soothe him, but it wasn't helping. Just thinking about that time in his life angered and agitated him.

"Tell me about it Lucas. I know you don't want to, but there can't be any secrets between us," Kaylee pleaded, and Lucas knew she was right.

"I was only eighteen when it happened. I was so full of myself," Lucas said, shaking his head. "I was the Guardian and a strong shifter. I had already started to feel my Alpha power and foolishly thought nothing could touch me. Marcus sent me to retrieve a package in New Orleans. He said now that I was a man, I could do more for the pack than just sitting around, taking up space." Luke heard Kaylee gasp, but when she didn't say anything, he continued.

"Yeah, he's always been an ass, but I was determined to prove myself to him. My youthful optimism made me think I could change my father's view of me if I completed his task. I didn't ask many questions, just where was I supposed to go and what I was picking up.

"He told me I was meeting a man by the name of Bane Walker who was supposed to give me an envelope I needed to bring back to the pack. Marcus gave me one night to complete the task. I didn't have a car or any money even though I'd been working odd jobs since I became a teen. Everything anyone in the pack made went right back to the pack, more specifically, to my father.

"It was another one of Marcus' lessons; if I was truly a man, I could figure out my own way to complete his assigned task. New Orleans wasn't that far away, four-and-a-half to five-hours by car, but since I didn't have one, I shifted and ran as long as I could in my wolf form. When I got too tired, or the area was too populated, I hitchhiked. It took forever.

"By the time I made it to the meeting place, no one was there. I found a place nearby to sit down and sleep for a little while it was still dark, and like I said, I was feeling very sure of myself."

"Oh no, Lucas, that was so dangerous," Kaylee said, looking back up at him. "I haven't been to New Orleans, but even I know there are parts tourists are encouraged to stay away from."

Lucas ran his hand down her head, encouraging her to lay it back on his chest. He didn't like thinking about that time of his life and his failures. It would be harder to tell the rest of the story if she was looking at him.

"Kaylee, I was stupid and cocky. What could anyone steal from me? I had nothing to give, maybe three whole dollars in my pocket. My clothes were nothing to attract attention, and I figured if anyone tried to hurt me, my Were strength would take care of that."

Lucas could feel Kaylee's head nodding on his chest, but she didn't move or say anything, just waited for him to tell her the rest.

"So, like I said, I was sleeping in an alley way when I felt hands pulling at me. I fought, but there were so many, and they were as strong as I was; I couldn't get away. They pinned me to the ground and that's when Bane Walker came up, standing over me.

"Marcus had sheltered me from the ways of the Others. I only knew of the Witches and our kind and hadn't even heard talk of Others. One look from the man who I later found out was Bane Walker, and my body froze. I couldn't move or look away from the man. I noticed his fangs, and I knew he was a vampire. He grabbed my shirt and pulled me toward him. It freaked me the fuck out, but I was frozen, I couldn't even lift a finger. When he bit me, it was like being struck by a snake, fast, but damn the pain was horrible. The asshole drained all the blood from my body, and I could feel the coldness creeping in. When I felt the last pump of my heart, he ripped open his wrist and placed it in my mouth, forcing me to swallow his blood. As I laid there, he threw an envelope on my chest and said, Your blood is strong with power, thank you for the taste. Fuck, Kaylee, he smiled at me with my blood still dripping from his fangs. It scared the shit out of me, but he wasn't done. If you make it through the transition, come and find me, your power will be too great for the pack."

"Jeezus, what did you do?" Kaylee asked.

"The first few days were horrible, fighting my two halves as they fought my body. Then the hunger, Kaylee, I can't even explain it, the need for blood was so strong, I didn't even think. I wandered half-crazed, not really knowing what was going on. There was a man who was attacking a woman, and hell, Kaylee, I killed him. I yelled at the woman to run. Once I knew she was gone, I drained him. He wasn't the only one."

"Lucas?"

"No, Kaylee, I told you, this part of me is dark. It's a time I've tried to make up for. Part of being a vampire is knowing a person's deepest, darkest thoughts, and even though those men were planning to hurt people, it didn't give me the right to kill them. I was out of control. It took me about a week to get back to the pack. I was freaked out and scared, and I naively thought my father would help me. When I got there, and he saw what had happened to me, he tried to have me banished. Your Grandma Ruth stepped in and wouldn't allow it."

"But he set you up," Kaylee protested as she got up on her knee and looked down at Lucas. "He sent you to that man. He had to have known what would happen." Lucas smiled at the outrage Kaylee was feeling on his behalf.

"That's the thing, I can't prove it. He told the pack I was out partying. I'm the only one who knew he sent me. He made sure to cover his tracks. When I confronted him, the asshole laughed and said, Prove it. Weres and Vampires never work together."

"What! What about the envelope?"

"There wasn't anything in it, and on the outside, someone had written, Debt Paid."

"Holy shit. How did you find out the vampire was Bane Walker?"

"When Marcus tried to banish me and it didn't work, he made living with the pack unbearable. I went back to New Orleans to track Bane down to get some answers. We fought, but he wouldn't give me anything, only his name, unless I allowed him to become my master. That shit wasn't happening. Up until that point, I had allowed myself to be led by Marcus and my need for acceptance; there was no way in hell I was going to let another person control me just to confirm my father had set me up.

"It took me three years to control the vampire side of me, so I could go back to the pack. I'm still an outsider, one they need, but that hasn't stopped Marcus from trying to find other ways to get rid of me."

"Oh, Lucas I'm so sorry you had to go through any of that."

Lucas was going to kiss her, but he sensed his brother coming in, fast. "Get up, babe, we're about to have company." Kaylee jumped up and gathered her clothes. Lucas was extremely thankful someone had thought ahead, bringing some of her things to the cabin because he had destroyed the clothes she was wearing when they first arrived.

Being naked or being seen naked wasn't a big deal for Were, so he knew his brother wouldn't say anything to him, but Kaylee was still new to all of this. Grabbing the jeans he had retrieved from the pond the night before, he slipped them on, not bothering with a shirt or shoes, and walked out the door. Matt was there seconds later.

"You need to come with me. It's bad, Luc. Marcus went off the hinges and attacked Flynn and Danica."

"We need to get Kaylee to her grandparents. We can deal with the pack after my mate is safe." Lucas didn't wait for his brother's agreement, just went back into the house and gathered up Kaylee. She asked a couple of questions and he answered them, leaving out some things. He could tell she knew something bad was up, but didn't want her to worry. She had a confrontation of her own to deal with.

Chapter 16

Kaylee walked into her grandparents' home, feeling very different from when she'd left. She was worried about Lucas and what was going on with his pack. Kaylee had only gotten bits and pieces of the conversation he had with Matt outside the door at the cabin, but none it of sounded good. When he told her she needed to go back to her grandparents' home, she didn't hesitate because she knew he needed to focus on what needed to be done and not on her.

Lucas had explained so much to her about her birthright and his. He also made her see she needed to speak with her Grandma Ruth and repair the rift which had developed between them. Kaylee was okay with that as long as her grandma didn't continue lying to her.

When she walked in the front door, Kaylee was bewildered to see both her grandparents sitting in the living room, as if they had been waiting for her. For as long as she could remember, they never sat in that room unless they had guests, there wasn't even a television. They were sitting on the couch, leaving on the loveseat the only other place to sit, which would put her right in front of them. Looked like she wasn't the only one who needed to have this conversation. Kaylee sat down and waited to see who would start. It was her Grandma Ruth, but she didn't apologize or give any further explanation. She began with what Kaylee wasn't willing to talk about, Lucas.

"You were with him, are you mated?" her grandma asked, sounding a bit angry and a lot disappointed.

"What I do with Lucas is my business. But I'll tell you this much, we are not mated, yet. If I have my way, that will change very soon, but Lucas refuses to until after my Ostara ceremony. I thought with your ability to know all, you would have already known that, Grandmother."

"At least one of you is showing some sense," her grandpa answered, his words cutting Kaylee like a knife. "McClane witches do not mix seeds with half-breeds. You will taint this line if you go through with this mating, spoiling future generations to come with your actions."

Kaylee put her head down resting her chin on her chest and took a couple of deep breaths. She needed to answer her grandpa in a very adult fashion when what she wanted to do was rage at his prejudice. Kaylee leaned forward, placing her elbows on her knees, then looked up at both her grands, the two people in this world who, up until three days ago, meant the most to her.

"I don't care what you think, either of you, Grandpa," Kaylee said, first looking at him, then her Grandma Ruth. "We're going to have to agree to disagree on this matter because my feelings won't change. Lucas is my mate, and we will complete the mating, binding us together. Now, I think you both owe me an explanation. I'm willing to sit here and hear you out, but if you lie to me again or try one of the other ways you've been manipulating me my entire life, I'm out of here, and you won't see me again."

"You can't do that," Grandma Ruth screeched, jumping up from the couch. "The Ostara is only a few short days away. You'll be vulnerable if you're not brought into your magic in the right way. The dark will be more tempting than you know, Kaylee, you need your family during this time. Lucas can't help you with this, for him to even try is foolhardy. It will destroy you both, mark my words."

"Well, then, I suggest you start talking. How about we start with my mother and why she decided, and you let her, to have me bound? Why for years she took me to therapists and doctors when she knew what I was seeing was real. Why don't we start there, Grandmother?"

She watched as her Grandma Ruth sat back down on the couch, slumping into it. Kaylee didn't like seeing her that way, but she needed answers, and Lucas would only give her so much. No, the answers she was seeking needed to come from these two people, then she would deal with her Mother.

Grandma Ruth looked up, and Kaylee could see the sheen of tears in her eyes, making her rethink everything. She didn't want to hurt her grands, but she had a right to know, didn't she?

"I should have told you when you were younger. I warned your mother this might happen, and that you needed to be prepared, not shielded, but she had other ideas. Nothing is black and white Kaylee. I respected your Mother's wishes, but I was always there for you. Part of my magic is empathy, I can see and feel things, especially when the person I'm channeling is close to me. I knew you, at a very young age, also possessed this power and wanted to start training you on how to deal with it. Your own emotions are hard, but adding other people to the mix is even more difficult.

"Your mother refused; she also possesses the trait and hates it. She didn't want you to deal with it. When she tried to bind you herself and the bind failed, she came to me, and I had no choice. The damage was already done and there was no reversing it. She used a spell with an expiration date, something the McClane witches have never done. If you invoke a time or date, then it cannot be undone. That's why we only provide general time frames, something you'll learn as you read the grimoire and start to understand your magic better."

"Why did she do it, why didn't she want me to know any of this, only to be blindsided right before my birthday?" Kaylee asked, resigned. She believed her Grandma Ruth had fought for her to know about her magic, but was forced into a decision she didn't like or agree with.

"Kaylee, only she can answer that question for you. In my opinion, it was fear. She never embraced her magic the way she should have. She didn't like feeling or seeing things which couldn't be explained or touched. Your mother needs to control things, and magic is fluid. Then there's your father."

"What does my father have to do with any of this? I don't even know him. Hell, Mom said he was dead."

"Your mom decided, much like you have, love is more important than family tradition or rules. Your father is very much alive. He is a warlock, one who has been banished from the Coven and not allowed to be a part of our family. Your mother ignored that and married him, anyway. That's why she stayed away and sent you to visit by yourself. She isn't in good standing with the Coven."

"I don't understand. Why was he was banished, what could he have possibly done? Mom never said a bad word about him, just that he couldn't deal with being a part of a family and needed to get away. She always told me he loved me, and it was better for me this way. When I got older and asked, she told me she had found out he had died."

Kaylee was starting to see a pattern she didn't like, every part of her life—her childhood, her parents, her grandparents—it was all filled with lies and betrayal.

"Kaylee, there is so much you don't know. He was banished from the Coven for being a warlock and using dark magic; even a small dose of dark magic can turn a witch evil. That was something the McClanes and the Smiths disagreed about. They felt as long as the witch only dabbled, it was okay; it's not, dark and light shouldn't mix. The McClanes and Smiths never did see eye to eye on that aspect of magic.

"As I was saying, your mom loved him and would do anything to be with him, despite what we said. I knew there was more going on than what met the eye, but I couldn't detect any dark magic at play. I only knew their relationship evolved too quickly. From almost the first moment they met, I started to see changes in Rebecca."

"Remind you of anyone?" Grandpa Edwin piped in his two cents, and Kaylee gave him a dirty look which, thankfully, shut him up for the moment.

"Please, Grandma Ruth, continue the story," Kaylee pleaded.

"Fine, child, but you're not going to like it any more than what I've already told you. As I said, they married and moved away. Your father insisted your mother have no contact with us, so we didn't even know about you until you were close to five-years old."

"What?" Kaylee's mind was spinning. She didn't have the first recollection of her father, but she remembered coming here at a very young age and staying with her grandparents. What Grandma Ruth was saying didn't make sense.

"I know what you're thinking child, and yes, we made sure you didn't remember your father and had memories of us. It made it easier after we finally got you away from that man. You wouldn't allow any of us, including your mother, to come near you. It was the only thing we could find to help soothe you and start to repair the damage he had done by taking you."

"Taken me, where the hell did he take me, Grandma? Hell, it's like I have a whole strange, unknown history. What you're saying doesn't make sense. If he was so bad why didn't Mom say so?"

"Let me finish. After a few years, your mom couldn't handle the dark man he had become. She had no choice but to leave, but he refused to allow you to go with her. She never embraced her magic and wasn't strong enough to fight him. He had charmed her into thinking it was the best thing for you at the time. He was a charmer in many ways.

"Somehow, she was able to break the hold he had over her and leave. She stayed away from you and the coven for five years. Your father told her she was never allowed to come within fifty miles of you, or he would put you on the path of dark magic. She was scared, still young, and because she had chosen him over the Coven or her family, ashamed to ask for help. But something happened which changed her mind, and she finally did the right thing and contacted me.

"Before you ask, I don't know, only your mother and father know the details. What I can tell you is he offered me no resistance when I came to collect you. You were living with him in Nome, Alaska, in a very tiny house which had seen better days. He had changed over the years and no longer had the handsome facade your mother had fallen for so fast. You were just a tiny thing and so scared. I gave you the tea for the first time that day, just to get you on the plane without screaming."

"Where is he now, is he still in Alaska? If he gave me up, does it mean he stopped practicing dark magic and is a better person? Do you think he would talk to me now?"

"Kaylee, I can't answer those questions. I do know he did stop practicing Wicca after you left; it was a condition the Coven placed on him. After that, he went into hiding. I believe it was to repent for the evil things he had done while under the influence of the dark ways. He still has many powers, is very powerful in his own right, but he refuses to use them. He promised me he would never do anything to hurt you. He also told me to tell your mother he was sorry for everything he had put her through."

"This is a lot to take in." Kaylee couldn't sit still, so she got up and started pacing the room. "Adding all of this to the magic, Were, and vampire stuff, my brain is about ready to explode. Hell, I think if one more thing happens, it just might. Lucas is at the pack house right now dealing with something his father has done and then all this."

"What's going on at the pack house?" This time her Grandpa Edwin didn't snark or make any snide comments. Mentioning Lucas and a problem at the pack house seemed to worry him.

"I don't know," Kaylee answered as honestly as she could. "Matt came to the cabin and said they needed Lucas back there. They went outside and talked for a bit, and then Lucas and Matt came back inside and told me I needed to get here, but they wouldn't let me come alone. They watched me from the trail until I was in the house. I'm scared though, I have a feeling whatever it is, it's awful, and Lucas could get hurt."

Grandpa Edwin didn't miss a beat. Much like Lucas had done, he started issuing orders, first to her grandma.

"You stay here and protect Kaylee. I'll go check out what's happening at the pack house. If the power shifts before the Ostara is complete, we are going to have even more problems. There'll be no stopping them if he comes into his Alpha powers. We'll be right back where we were when Rebecca decided to leave and ignore the Coven."

Kaylee knew her grandpa had issues with her and Lucas, and after hearing about her parents, she also now knew why, but this was different. She and Lucas were different; he wasn't evil or practicing dark magic, he was the Guardian. He also loved her, and she loved him with her whole heart. The realization slammed into her like a Mack truck. She loved him.

She watched her grandpa leave. He no longer looked like the frail, little man she had come to think he was, but a warrior. That's when she realized a glimmer surrounded him. Shit, just another deception to add to the list.

"Kaylee, there's still more I need to tell you, to prepare you for, Grandma Ruth said.

"Enough," Kaylee said. After she knew Lucas was safe and what was going on at the pack house, she would deal with her destiny. "Grandma, I think I've heard about as much as I can take for now, can we continue this later?"

"Kaylee, do not take this lightly, you have a big decision to make on your birthday," Grandma demanded

The tone of her voice grated on Kaylee's nerves. She thought she'd been taking all of this relatively well and hated when anyone talked down to her like she was a child.

"I know, Grandma," she snapped. "I just really don't want to think about it right now. I think I deserve that much after what all of you have done to me, kept from me all these years. I'll deal with the magic portion of my life after this part is finished. Is that too much to fucking ask?"

Her grandma Ruth looked sheepish and ashamed of herself, but of course, didn't apologize or offer any type of acknowledgment.

"See that you do. This can't wait, time is running short," Grandma Ruth warned and walked out of the living room, leaving Kaylee alone with her thoughts and worries. It was the first time she considered calling her grandma a bitch.

Chapter 17

Lucas and Matt waited until Kaylee was safely in grandparents' home. Once she was inside, Lucas asked, "What's going on, why would Marcus hurt Danica?" He didn't bother to ask about Flynn because Marcus was a twisted fuck who was always causing the Omega of their pack problems and pain.

Lucas could tell Matt was agitated, he was pacing back and forth and running his hands though is hair. His brother was struggling with something much bigger than Marcus going off on the pack; through the years, it was a common occurrence. The only reason Lucas was even remotely concerned this time was Danica had never been one of Marcus's targets. The females in the pack were meant to be cherished.

"Fuck, listen, Marcus has been drinking Dragons Blood."

Lucas grabbed Matt by his shirt, getting right up in his face and yelled, "What the fuck, Matt, and you didn't say anything to anyone? You fucking know if the council finds out you knew about this and didn't say anything, you could be put down, right?"

Lucas pushed Matt away and turned around, he couldn't look at him right now. Dragon's Blood was a potion made by the users of dark magic. If a Were even tasted a drop, they got an instant high, becoming addicted, giving the maker of the substance rule over the Were drinking it. Those dark magic users either used the power themselves or sold it off to the highest bidder. That's why the council had banned it.

"You think I don't know that!" Matt yelled grabbing Lucas' arm and making him turn to face him. "Up until last month, I believed everything the man said. When he said he could handle it, I believed him. He wasn't acting any differently and hell, I didn't even know about the fucking money he was taking from the pack."

"Bullshit, Matt, you just didn't want to see it. You liked the position Marcus put you in, the favored son, the prince who could do no wrong and got away with everything. What did it cost you to turn a blind eye to everything he's done?"

"Fuck you, Lucas, I'm trying to make up for it now. I didn't know."

"Again, I call bullshit. You're running scared now that he's out of control and his actions are going to cost you. So, just like the spoiled brat you've always been, you want the rest of us to clean up the mess." Lucas laughed, but without humor. "He told you one day you would be Alpha, didn't he? That bastard was never going to give up his throne. He would rather kill all of us than ever allow that to happen. You weren't special, you were a fucking pawn, so he could get away with his shit. He needed a strong member of the pack to have his back, and you filled the position with a smile on your face."

"Fine, I was stupid, I believed everything he promised and said. Are you fucking happy? This is all my fault."

"No, Matt, I'm not fucking happy, I'm pissed. You could have said something, we could have done something, and none of this would be happening now. Do you think I like any of this shit? I'm not ready to be Alpha and neither are you." Lucas felt bad for Matt, he wanted to console him, but his next words stopped him.

"That's not all of it, Lucas. He gave Emily the Dragons Blood because she wasn't willing to pay his debt. It messed her up, but whoever Marcus owes messed her up worse. When Dani said there was too much damage, he freaked the fuck out and hit her."

"Son of a bitch! I'll deal with you later. Right now, the pack is what's important," Lucas said as he started running. Knowing time was critical, he used his vampire speed and arrived at the pack house well before Matt. When he arrived, Eric, Macon, and Dylan were standing off against Marcus, all of them in wolf form.

The fight was brutal. Marcus was using his strength as Alpha against his pack mates, but the men weren't standing down. Lucas admired their strength and determination, but he knew it was only a matter of time before Marcus would take them down. Lucas didn't even hesitate, he ripped his clothes off and shifted as he ran to join the fight, charging Marcus head on. Lucas was strong, but Marcus was hyped up on Dragon's Blood, making him almost invincible. Matt joined him a few minutes later, and together, they managed to beat him back.

He and Matt took turns attacking, but it was getting them nowhere because they couldn't kill Marcus. This wasn't an Alpha challenge, there were rules which needed to be followed. To take the kill shot, Lucas and Matt needed the pack's approval or the Council would come after them, and Matt was already in enough trouble. The pack needed to know what Marcus had done, everything.

Lucas shifted back into his human form. It was a risk, Marcus could tear him apart in his fragile human skin, but it was a risk Lucas needed to take. He needed to get the man to shift back into his human form, and Lucas knew if he goaded him, Marcus' ego would win out over his need to cause pain.

Lucas stood his ground, and Matt came next to him, still in his wolf form. He noticed Eric and Dylan had flanked Marcus and Macon was at his back. The pack had him surrounded which gave Lucas a small amount of confidence this move would work.

"Marcus, shift back and face me as a man," Lucas demanded. Marcus shifted, and Lucas instantly noticed his eyes, the gold color of the animal dull and the surrounding ring which should have been blue, was pitch black, proving the taint of dark magic had been firmly planted within him.

"Face, you like a man?" Marcus laughed. "Since when have you ever been a man, whelp? You're nothing, but what I made you, weak. Even with your brother at your side, you're still weak. I made sure of that when I broke the twin bond early. King Alpha's, born as twin souls on the day of the red moon. I called bullshit then, and I call it now. You are nothing, he is nothing, unless I choose it. I am Alpha of the Valentin pack, you are the scum who disgraces our pack name."

"I'm the scum of the Valentin pack, huh?" Lucas scoffed. "Have you taken a good look in the mirror lately, Father? How was that last dose of Dragons Blood? Did it make you feel good?" Lucas noticed the twitch on the side of Marcus's eye; he also noticed he was looking around at the pack, mainly at Eric who had now shifted back to human form as well. Lucas wasn't done, there was still one more nail he needed to pound into Marcus's coffin.

"How did Emily take it when you forced her to drink it? Do you think she felt good?" Lucas heard Eric's howl of pain and disgust, but he couldn't look away from Marcus. He needed to keep his focus on the man who was hell bent on ruining them because, on a good day, the bastard was unpredictable. With Dragons' Blood running through his veins, he was even more of a threat to the pack. Lucas knew Marcus would do anything to protect his own ass even if it meant killing every single one of them to keep his secret.

"Oh, that's what you've resorted to now, lies?" Marcus laughed. "You think the pack will believe I would ever allow that type of taint to corrupt this pack? No, you're the abomination, not me; they know, I've told them. They see you for the evil creature you are."

"The evil creature you made sure I became, isn't that what you should be saying, Father?"

"More lies to cover for yourself, Lucas. I shouldn't be surprised, you've always been a coward. Maybe it's you who is taking Dragon's Blood, and now that the little witch is here, you need to distract everyone. I'll show them though, I'll prove the witches chose the wrong Guardian."

"And who should they have chosen as Guardian, Father?"

"The pure Alpha of the Valentin Pack," Marcus snarled, "not the weak imitation."

"You? The man who works with their enemy? The man who willingly allows another to control and rule his mind? You think you're the rightful Guardian? Where is this purity you speak of so fondly? All I see is a jealous, hateful man. The pack will not stand behind you this time, Father. Your game has been lost, you will be judged by the Council for your actions."

"Lies, all lies. I should have put you down before your first breath, and I would have if that bitch hadn't interfered. Now, I'm done, I'm done playing this game. The witches aren't here to protect you, and I don't see a single member of the Council standing around ready to investigate your claim. The pack will back me when I say you challenged me for Alpha and lost, and I will finally be rid of you. They'll be forced to choose another Valentin to act as Guardian, and that will be me!"

"The only person who is lying is you, Father." Matt had stepped up next to Lucas, having shifted back. "I won't stand by your side and lie, neither will the pack. Your time as the Valentin Alpha has come to an end; you are not worthy of the name." Before Matt got another word from his lips, Marcus charged him, but Lucas pushed him out of the way.

Lucas had Marcus down on the ground. He still couldn't kill him, but he needed time to come up with another plan.

"Get off me, boy" Marcus, groaned as he threw him with the grip he had around Lucas' neck. Lucas felt his beast coming to the surface; he

108

had to fight it as well as his Father. When he got up from where he had been thrown, Lucas shifted. Marcus had already shifted after slinging Lucas off him. Marcus's wolf was somewhat smaller than Lucas, grey in color, with black eyes. Lucas let out a haunting howl and rammed into his father's wolf, knocking him off his feet, grabbing him by the throat. Before the fight went any further, there was a loud clap of thunder and a bolt of lightning landed right beside them. Everything had stopped. Marcus was sitting on the ground, not far from him, and Edwin was standing over him.

"I am the Warlock of the McClane coven; I am also on the Council. I have heard the charges against you, Marcus Valentin, and I find you guilty. You have been trying to destroy this pack for years, but we've been unable to step in. Dragon Blood taints your soul now. I have called for the enforcers, and you will stand before the Council and accept your fate."

"Lucas, you are the next in line for Alpha of the Valentin Pack. If your pack mates agree, they need to break the bond with Marcus, now. He cannot be allowed to hold that power any longer," Edwin advised still holding Marcus with his magic. "If they choose to stay with Marcus as leader, they will be taken down with him, and the Valentin pack will be destroyed."

Lucas looked around the yard; every member of the pack was there. Danica and Emily were off to the side, holding on to each other. Noticing the bruises on both women made Lucas want to fight his father all over again. Eric, Dylan, and Macon were still standing guard, making sure no one left the circle. Flynn was back further, just as bruised as the girls. Lucas could see the tears in the man eyes, and it broke a part of him.

Lucas knew Flynn would take Marcus' betrayal personally. He was the Omega, it was his job to calm the pack and keep it together, but Marcus had never let him. It would take time for Flynn to recover from what was happening. Lucas was astonished when Flynn was the first pack member to step forward.

"I, Flynn Valentin, Omega of the Valentin, denounce you Marcus as my Alpha and sever all ties."

Lucas watched as Marcus started screaming, the pain of the bonds breaking as one after the other repeated the same saying. When it came to his and Matt's turn, they chanted the saying together, using their power as one for the first time in their lives.

"We twins, born King Alphas of the Valentin Pack break all ties by blood and by bond to Marcus, former Alpha of the Valentin pack."

Lucas felt the bonds break, feeling freer than he had ever felt, but then something else started to happen. New bonds formed in his body. He felt Eric, strong and formable, Danica's sweet and loving nature, Flynn's warmth and calm, Dylan and Macon's protectiveness, and even Emily's sass. He felt them all, then he felt Matt. Just as strong as himself, but wary.

"The pack has chosen," Edwin's voice boomed over the yard. "Lucas Valentin, you are the new Alpha of the Valentin Pack. Guard them well." Edwin raised his staff and spoke words Lucas didn't understand. Marcus was screaming his head off, threatening every one of them with revenge. Seconds later, it was all quiet, only the pack remained; Edwin and Marcus had disappeared.

Lucas looked around, not knowing what to do next. The pack had chosen him to be the Alpha. Matt once again reclaimed the spot at Lucas' side.

"You know this isn't over yet. If Marcus can find a way, he'll be back and gunning for you and Kaylee. Edwin is strong, but Marcus has been playing this game for a long time. If he's able to fool the Council, he'll come after all of us."

Lucas looked out at the pack. They had all come closer, and he knew he needed to say something.

"You have chosen me as Alpha. I will give all of you one chance to rescind your bond without repercussions. We have a fight coming our way. The guardianship must still be honored and the Ostara must proceed, but Marcus sold his soul. We need to find out to whom because they will be coming, and we need to be prepared."

Emily tried to step forward, but stumbled, so Danica helped her. "His Master is Bane Walker," she said crying, "he did this to me. He wants the Blue Moon Priestess and all her power. Marcus told him how to get it."

"Fuck!" Lucas yelled. "Eric protect the pack, I need to find my mate."

"Your mate?" The pack all echoed back to him.

"Kaylee," Lucas yelled over his shoulder, "the Blue Moon Priestess is my mate and Alpha female to this pack. She must be protected at all costs!"

Kaylee had been waiting at the door for Lucas to come back. When she saw him coming into the yard, she ran to him, jumping into his arms.

"Are you okay?"

"Yeah, babe, I'm fine, but we need to talk."

Kaylee hated those words. She could see the worry on Lucas' beautiful face and wanted to take it away.

"Tell me."

"I'm Alpha; my father has been banished, taken to the Council. He was taking Dragon's Blood." Kaylee looked at him funny, she didn't have the first clue what he was talking about. "I'll tell you about it later. Babe, we need go to the pack house. It's bad, but I can't leave them or you alone right now. My maker is after you. Now, with Marcus gone and out from under his control, he'll retaliate."

"I'll do whatever you need, whatever we have to do."

"Congratulations, Alpha," Grandma Ruth said, walking out into the yard. "It's about time you took your rightful place."

Both Kaylee and Lucas were startled at her words, but didn't have a chance let them sink in.

"This is how it was always meant to be," she shocked them even further. "Marcus was destroying the pack, but until you decided to take his place, there was nothing any of us could do, Lucas. You need to know what's coming, what you have to prepare for. You have a brother, his name is Atticus. He is a hybrid just like you, but he's stronger. He's been training for this day his entire life. With the black magic running in his body, he's Bane's biggest accomplishment and yet, his biggest rival."

"What?" Kaylee and Lucas questioned.

"Atticus belonged to another pack from Mississippi, but was also lured to New Orleans by Bane who turned him the same way he turned you, Lucas. Only Atticus accepted Bane's bargain.

"Bane is nothing more than a ruthless vampire feeding off young guys on the dirty streets of New Orleans," Lucas said. "Why would anyone go along with what he offered, give up their very soul?"

Lucas remembered all the times Bane had tried to summon Luc. Over time, he was able to resist. He had become stronger, and with the help of Ruth, they had found a way to block his pleas.

"Not everyone is like you, and I can't answer for Atticus. What I will tell you is his time of reckoning is coming. He'll need to make a choice, but that's his story to live and to tell if he so wishes."

"Everything is like a fucking riddle," Kaylee screamed. "Why can't it just be black and white with an outcome we can fight or prepare for? There are so many what ifs and if onlys, it makes my head spin."

"I know child," Grandma Ruth hugged her close, "but there is no other way. The fates have a plan, and we're just along for the ride.

"Go to your pack, help them heal, and enjoy life while you can. We only have days until the ceremony. I will come to you, Kaylee, to prepare you the best I can, but your focus needs to be on the pack and building your life with Lucas. That will be your greatest strength." Grandma Ruth walked away, leaving Lucas and Kaylee alone, holding one another.

Kaylee looked up at Lucas and said, "Ready to introduce me to your family?"

Lucas smiled, "Anytime, babe."

Chapter 18

Kaylee was still in a state of shock four days later as she looked through the McClane family's grimoire. It was more than just a spell book, it was a history of the family. Kaylee knew on the night of her Ostara, she would be blessed with the knowledge inside the book, but that was hard to take in. One day she would be completely human, well not completely, and the next she would be a witch with all the powers and knowledge to go along with it.

That's why it was important for all the family members to attend. Any knowledge gained would be passed down through the Mother Goddess to the recipient. This time, the recipient would be Kaylee. It also explained that although she would retain the knowledge of the entire McClane Coven, she would have to learn how to use those skills. Her Grandmother had been talking her though some of the simpler ones, but Kaylee felt inept and clueless. It was frustrating; without her magic, everything was just hypothetical.

"You can read and learn all you want," was Grandma's simple answer to her frustration, "but without hard work, comprehension, and skill, none of it will mean anything in the end. It's your choice to complete the tasks and travel the road you have chosen. I can give you the basics, but the rest is up to you."

Kaylee had also figured out her Grandma Ruth hadn't exactly been ignoring her training all these years. When they started discussing the herbs and plants within the book, Kaylee was already well aware of them—what they looked like, what they smelled like, and the legend behind them. It had been a game for years between the two of them and without the special tea clouding her mind, much of those memories were coming back to her.

But there was still a part of her which couldn't believe all of this was happening. She wanted to yell and scream, maybe even freak out a little, but that wouldn't do any of them any good or change the facts. Lucas was a Hybrid, Grandma Ruth, the High Priestess, her Grandpa a Warlock, and Kaylee, she was going to be the Blue Moon Priestess. A witch with immense power. Damn. It all scared the shit out of her.

She had been reading for a few hours and came across an entry in the book which spoke to her above all others. You will never understand how much power and information is forced upon you. It is overwhelming, life altering, and scary. I have been preparing for this day my entire life, and yet, nothing I learned or practiced came close to reality. I cannot help but question if this is right. Why has the Mother Goddess chosen us to carry this magic? Why are we so special? Rebecca McClane.

As if the grimoire had conjured her from Kaylee's thoughts, her mother was standing in the doorway, looking like she always did, completely composed and polished, not a single blonde hair out of place in her stylish bun. Her pantsuit pressed to perfection and her makeup impeccably placed on her smooth, wrinkle-free skin. The only unusual thing about her mother was the way she was wringing her hands together as if she was nervous. She should be, this was a long time coming.

"Kaylee?"

"Hello, Mother, what are you doing here? Come to watch me fail or is it that you think I may choose the path my father did? My, surprisingly, alive father" Kaylee asked shutting the grimoire and pushing the book out of her way, not bothering to get up. There would be no warm hugs or kiss on the cheek as she had done with Grandma Ruth when she arrived. No, Kaylee just leaned back in her chair and crossed her arms over her chest, waiting for her mother to speak.

"Your Grandma called and said you needed me. So, I came."

"No, she didn't, but that's probably because I told her not to invite you." Kaylee watched as her mother flinched at her words. There was a small part of her which thought she would get some satisfaction by hurting her, like Kaylee had been hurt, but she didn't.

"Kaylee, listen, you don't understand, things were different for me. I just wanted you to experience a normal life before all this took hold," her mother said, waving her hand at the book on the table.

"All this, you mean my heritage? Or the magic?"

"Kaylee, please, I just wanted to see how you were dealing with it all and to support you through your Ostara."

"With it all, hmm, do you mean that my entire family, which up until a couple of days ago consisted of you, me, Grandma, and Grandpa, now includes multiple cousins, aunts, and uncles? Or are you asking how I'm dealing with the fact the man I love is a hybrid Were/Vampire? Oh, wait, don't answer that because this is an even better question. Are you asking how I'm dealing with the fact my own mother lied to me, made me think there was something wrong with me, sent me to doctors, put me on medications, all because of the legacy she gave me at birth? Oh no, wait, how about that you insisted my own grandmother drug me and bind my powers, so I could lead this so-called normal life? Feel free to answer any of those questions mother, I would be really interested in your answers."

Her mother sighed, but walked into the room, taking the seat across from Kaylee at the table. "I never wanted you to fail, Kaylee, never that. I just wanted you to have a choice."

"A choice? I don't know, Mother, according to Grandma Ruth there are really only two choices, light or dark." Kaylee sat there for a minute and then realized what her mother was talking about. "You didn't want me to have a choice, you wanted me to deny this part of me, didn't you?" Kaylee accused. "That's why you sent me to all those doctors, made me take all those pills, you wanted me to stay human."

"Kaylee, one thing you'll find out with age is that you are not infallible, you'll make mistakes, some of them small and some you can't apologize enough for, but you're right. I wanted you to deny this part of you. I thought if you didn't realize what was going on, your twenty-fifth birthday would come and go, like any other day."

"How could you? That wasn't your choice to make, Mother, it was mine. You made me feel like I was crazy that there was something wrong with me. Didn't it even occur to you that I had absolutely no friends? Or the only time I was happy was while I was here? Of course, you didn't because work was more important than I was, your normal life, the life you wanted me to live. Only difference was you got to make your choice, didn't you?"

"Kaylee, you'll never truly understand, and I can't make you, but when you were a child, the magic you already held scared me. You were so powerful even then, and I knew if I didn't do something about it, those powers would only grow."

"Oh, I get being scared, Mother. I feel like I've spent most of my life that way."

"Kaylee, you were always so strong, not like me. I knew when you turned eighteen, I needed to step back and let you make the choices in your life. I couldn't let my fears rule your life."

"Oh, please, you're going to act as if just up and leaving your only child was a hardship or a choice to make my life better? Get real, you hadn't even taught me how to balance a checkbook or buy groceries so they lasted through the week. What you did was run. Seems like you're well-skilled at that, according to Grandma."

Her mother got up and started pacing. Kaylee figured she would leave soon, but was surprised when she started talking while she walked back and forth. "You know, you're so much like him. He was just as bullheaded and argumentative."

"Who, my father?"

"Yes, James," Kaylee's mom said with a little smile, "you're just like him. So stubborn and so damn strong. He's the reason your powers came in so early. Did your grandma tell you that? His family doesn't wait for the twenty-fifth birthday, they start ceremonies at birth. I wouldn't let him do that with you, but it didn't matter. He told me it would, but I didn't believe him. I was so stupid and naïve back then.

"He was so sure you were going to be this amazing witch, that you would lead our people into the next generation. That our family would be different that our love for each other and for you could conquer everything."

"Grandma said he tricked you, spelled you into going with him, being with him?"

"Your grandma has always wanted to believe in fairy tales, but I made choices. Choices she didn't agree with. It seems like each generation is plagued with that, aren't they?"

Kaylee didn't answer, she knew her mother didn't expect her to. "Tell me about him then, give me that much. You've always said good things about him, said he loved me, but nothing more." Kaylee realized something. "You loved him, didn't you?"

"Yes, I loved him very much."

"I don't understand, Grandma..."

"Your grandma doesn't know everything, Kaylee, just like I don't know everything about you. I wasn't spelled to be with your dad, I wanted him from the start. It was only after you were born that our problems started. He had started working with dark magic and it took him over. He did some things, things which scared me, and I tried to leave. He took measures to prevent it."

"So, he did compel you?"

"Yes, but the spell was easily broken. He actually made you the key."

Kaylee gasped. "By the tears of my sweet girl," she mumbled.

"Yes," her mother smiled, stopping in front of the table. "He made you his counter spell, every single time."

"I want to meet him," Kaylee stated emphatically.

"Kaylee, he won't see you. I don't know the whole story, but things happened when he left with you, things which scared even him. He'd always been fearless. The last time I saw him, he was weak. Whatever happened during that time broke him."

"Then we need to help him."

"He won't accept it, Kaylee, like I said stubborn and strong. So, did I hear you say you have a mate?"

"Mom, listen, I realize we're getting things out in the open and talking, but I don't know if I can just forgive everything which has happened. Everything you have put me through. We've never been close, so I'm not going to discuss my mate with you now."

"I get that, Kaylee, I just," she paused, then continued, "the Ostara ceremony means a new beginning for you. I was hoping it could be a new beginning for us as well."

Kaylee wanted that, but there was just so much hurt left in her. "Maybe, Mom, maybe." It would take time, but she hoped they could build something from here. Her mom wanting to help with her transition to a witch was a start. Admitting to being scared and all the past hurts also helped, but only time and effort, on both of their parts, would heal the wounds of the past. Kaylee just hoped her mother didn't run again, like every other time.

Chapter 19

Kaylee and Lucas began working together to help the pack heal. Kaylee knew it wouldn't happen overnight or that she would be accepted anytime soon. They were all too raw, but she liked them. Even the prickly Emily had some redeeming qualities.

Danica and Flynn were by far her favorites, they both had such kindness in them. Kaylee thought with all they had been through, they would be a little standoffish or jaded, but both of them welcomed her to the pack with open arms. Eric, on the other hand, was exactly what she expected. He watched her like a hawk. He even mentioned once if she hurt Lucas or the pack, she would have to deal with him.

Lucas had overhead the conversation and the two promptly went into fight mode. Kaylee hadn't even gotten a chance to stop it or say a word. One minute they were men and the next their wolves were fighting, tooth and claw. She hadn't liked it, hadn't liked being the cause of it. Lucas later explained it was the way of the pack. He was Alpha and although he wanted to be fair and just, there were times when he needed to make sure the pack knew exactly where he stood, and he had to put them in their place.

She was his mate, the Alpha female. At some time, she would need to show that, but until she was ready, he would be the one to make the pack understand. Kaylee was having a hard time with it; she didn't want to fight these people and felt it was more important to earn her place with kindness and understanding. It was a point she and Lucas disagreed on. She wasn't a shifter, so she didn't have the first clue on how to deal with the animals which laid beneath the surface. Danica and Lucas assured her, in time, she would figure it all out. She hoped they were right.

Dylan and Macon weren't overly friendly toward her, giving her a wide berth most times, but every once in a while, she saw through to their playful nature and even got a couple of jokes in at their expense. They both took it in stride and continued the play. Things were looking up for all of them, but they still had a long way to go before any of them completely accepted one another.

Emily was another matter altogether. She was hateful and mean most days, and Kaylee found herself wanting to slap her more than once. Conceding Emily was still dealing with the effects from the Dragon's Blood, she had cut her some slack.

Lucas explained it was like heroin mixed with dark magic. Kaylee had been working with her grands, learning all she could before the Ostara and understood how deadly the potion really was. It couldn't be detected by smell, taste, or touch, or even by a witch or warlock. It was also almost impossible to determine the maker or owner of the potion unless the person who made it was sloppy.

There was one spell which would expose the taint, but it was harmful to the recipient and so far, Ruth, Lucas, and Emily had all decided to wait and see what would happen. Emily had only had one dose, and according to her, it was small. Not that it mattered, the damage was already done.

Ruth had done a binding spell to, hopefully, keep Emily safe from whoever now owned her wolf's soul. Her grandma had explained it was like putting a band-aid on a gunshot wound. Nothing would free Emily unless her new Master released her or died.

Since taking over as Alpha, Lucas had been distracted with everything he needed to do for the pack. Marcus had nearly destroyed them in more ways than one. Their accounts were in the red, and they couldn't come up with a way to fix it without going to the council and asking for more, which rubbed Lucas the wrong way. He was a proud man and felt it was their responsibility to fix what they all had allowed to happen.

Flynn, Dylan, and Macon had offered a solution. For years, they had been hiding a small company they created from Marcus. Flynn made the most beautiful glass art Kaylee had ever seen. Some of his pieces were selling on an online site for as much as three thousand dollars apiece. Dylan and Macon, on the other hand, were buying up small lots of furniture and other odds and ends at auctions, refurbishing them, turning them into show pieces.

Eric had started investing their money and each of them had a healthy portfolio which they offered to the pack. Lucas turned them down at first, which Kaylee could tell hurt the four men. They wanted to provide for the pack as much as he did. Kaylee decided to put her time at the bank to use and came up with a business plan they all could agree on, creating a partnership. Lucas was an excellent carpenter in his own right and once they all sat down without the bad feelings between them, Valentin Furnishings and More was born.

Lucas' one requirement was they all contributed evenly. Kaylee knew the stipulation was put in place so the pack would feel equal and wouldn't be taken advantage of down the line. Lucas never wanted to stifle them like Marcus had done.

Kaylee had wanted to contribute and join in the company as well, but Lucas refused, saying his portion included her; since they were mates, everything he had, was hers. That rubbed her the wrong way, and they fought. Kaylee didn't want to be a kept woman, she wanted to work for their future as much as he did. She didn't have much, but she would give it without a second thought. When he refused, it hurt, but after talking with her Grandma Ruth, she decided to pick her battles. This was one she didn't think she would win; damn Alpha male.

So, she found other ways to contribute. Paying a bill when it came in without saying anything or buying groceries. She was the one who kept the books along with Eric, so no one was the wiser, and it made her feel good. Matt and Danica offered to work for them; everything was falling into place. Emily was the only standout, but again, Kaylee felt the poor woman had enough to deal with, and they all agreed to give her time.

Last night, Lucas had whisked her out of the pack house, blindfolding her; Kaylee loved the spontaneity of it and even the mystery. They had spent every night together in each other's arms, making love and talking, but this was different, special. She loved having him all to herself. As they walked hand in hand, Kaylee let him guide her, neither saying a word. As they were walking, she realized how much she trusted this man, how much she loved him.

When he guided her up some steps, she knew where they were, the cabin. She heard the door open and felt the pressure of Lucas' hand on her lower back, guiding her inside. When he removed the blindfold, Kaylee started to cry. Every available surface was covered with twinkling candles. He had a fire burning in the fireplace and a pallet of rose petal covered blankets in front of it, complete with a bottle of champagne chilling in a bucket of ice, and two crystal flutes. It was like something out of a dream.

Lucas stood behind her, holding her steady as she took it all in. One arm wrapped around her chest, the other around her waist, his thumb rubbing her belly in soft, soothing circles. Well, Kaylee guessed they were supposed to be soothing. Right now, she wanted nothing more than to strip them both bare and get on with the night he had so thoughtfully prepared for them.

"Lucas, this is so beautiful, thank you so much." Pulling away a little, so his arm loosened around her, she turned to face him, placing her arms around his shoulders.

"Anything for you, Kaylee," Lucas murmured as he nuzzled the top of her head with his cheek. "I wanted this day to be special. Tomorrow you'll come into your powers, but tonight I want us to come together as one."

Kaylee laughed, stroking his shoulders and neck. She was a little nervous and even a little scared. She knew exactly what he wanted to do, claim her. They'd been talking about it for a while now. She knew he would bite her and take her blood. She also knew to complete the claiming, she would need to take a little of his blood into her body, marking him as well. That scared her more than him taking from her, she didn't want to hurt him.

"Kaylee?" Lucas questioned as she remained quiet. "If you want to wait, I just thought..."

Kaylee didn't like the doubt and vulnerability she sensed in him. Lucas was a strong man, Alpha of his pack and Guardian to the McClane witches. He had lived through so many things and had not only survived, but thrived. Even this claiming was a testament to how much he had overcome. Just a few short weeks ago, the thought of taking her blood had made him run. She refused to allow her weakness to hurt him anymore.

"Claim me, Lucas, I'm yours, now and forever," she said, looking up into his beautiful blue eyes. "Whatever happens, I will always be by your side. Together we can do anything. You are my home, my love, and my future. I love you, Lucas Valentin, every part of you."

Kaylee watched as Lucas' eyes flashed bright gold seconds before his lips crashed into hers in a heated kiss which went on forever. Just when she was sure she was going to pass out from the pleasure, Lucas pulled away slightly, resting his forehead on hers, looking deeply into her eyes.

"I love you, Kaylee Smith, I think I have from the very moment I saw you driving down the dirt road. The dirt road might have had a different destination, but it led you to me, and I have never been happier. I love you, I cherish you, and I want you to be mine in every way. Do you accept me as your mate, Kaylee? Will you live and love by my side for all the days to come until we breathe our last breath together when the fates decide that day has come?"

Kaylee was crying, but she managed a croaked, "Yes, Lucas please make me yours, claim me."

Lucas grabbed her thighs, lifting her into his embrace. Hugging her closely, he walked the few steps to the pallet, laying her down gently, following her with his body. This time, their lovemaking was slow and sweet. Lucas took the time to explore every inch of her body, and Kaylee did the same.

Kaylee knew the time had come to complete the claim. Lucas was buried deep within her body. She could feel the beginning of her orgasm as it built so deeply within her, but she felt him hesitate. Looking up into his eyes, she cupped his cheek, bringing him closer, kissing him softly.

"I'm ready, Lucas, make me yours."

Her words seemed to spur him on; Lucas shifted his hip, his cock hitting her in just the right spot with every thrust. She could feel him growing inside her and knew exactly what she needed to do. Tilting her head to the side, exposing her neck to him, she offered herself to him, and he started to pound into her harder, deeper.

Just as she exploded around him, Lucas struck, biting her neck. Kaylee was so overwhelmed with pleasure, the slight pain only amplified her orgasm, making it stronger. He pulled his mouth away from her neck, and she looked at him. His eyes were completely gold, his fangs protruding over his lip. She watched as he let one of those razor-sharp teeth slice his lip. Kaylee pulled him down and licked the blood away, taking it into her body.

She was pleased by how good it tasted; it was sweet, yet harsh, so much like her Lucas. Sucking his lip into her mouth, she bit down, drawing more of his blood into her mouth. Seconds later, her body bowed under him as the claim and bond snapped into place. This was nothing like she was expecting because hell, there wasn't any way a person could describe it. She felt him inside her, in her heart, her brain, and her body. They were one on more than one level.

Lucas howled, and she felt the hot splash of his cum coating her womb, throwing her into another orgasm, this one so strong, she felt as though she was having an out-of-body experience. It took her forever to come back to earth, but when she did, Lucas was looking at her with as much love in his eyes as she had in her heart for him. It was done, they were mates.

Chapter 20

Kaylee was pleasantly sore from their activities the night before and that morning. Touching the tender skin on her neck, each little tingle of pain made her remember their claiming and brought a smile to her face. Lucas was hers and she was his.

Then there was this morning. Lucas had started her day by waking her up in the best possible way with his head between her legs. Then he had her ride him like a cowgirl and after she came three times, he took over, pinning her to the bed and giving her two more. She was still soaking up the afterglow when three women she had never seen before appeared in their bedroom. She had expected Lucas to jump up and defend her, but he only laughed, kissing her deeply.

"It looks like it's time for you to meet your family. Kayley, I would like to introduce you to your very rude and intrusive cousins, Amelia, Tara, and Prue."

Kaylee had gathered the sheet up to cover her body and could only stare at the three women. They looked a little like her—same shape and skin tone—but there were slight differences. Tara had strawberry blond hair and a mischievous look in her green eyes. Amelia's hair was closer to brown and cut short in a pixie cut which looked amazing with her dainty features and her hazel brown eyes; she looked to be the most serious of the group. The last one, Prue, had dark brown hair on the verge of being black, her eyes a soft brown. If Kaylee had to describe the woman by just looking, she would think sweet. The one thing they all had in common, including Kaylee, was the McClane nose and none of them would be considered small women, they all had curves for days.

"Now, Lucas, you knew we were coming," Amelia, who Kaylee was finding out was the ring leader, said, "and we did at least wait until the two of you stopped shaking the walls and screaming to the gods or in your case screaming each other's names. When Tara wanted to come in during your extracurriculars, shall we say, Prue and I overruled her. You should be grateful we waited."

Lucas went to get up. Kaylee was just starting to get used to the fact he had no problem with his nudity, but she didn't like the idea of these women, relations or not, seeing him in all his glory. She grabbed his arm and pulled him back down onto the bed, shoving a pillow over his groin, making him both bowl over from the force of her actions and laugh because he knew what she was up to.

"If you ladies would mind giving us a minute, I would like to get dressed first before you tell me why you decided to come into my home and more specifically, my bedroom without my permission," Kaylee said through clenched teeth.

Prue, the sweet one, said, "Certainly," but she had to pull Tara out of the room when she kept trying to steal a look. Amelia just walked out as if it wasn't a big deal.

"I like it when you get jealous, mate." Lucas tackled her to the bed. "I would show you how much if we had time, but you need to prepare, and I need to get with the pack to set up sentries. Tonight is the night, babe, you'll come into your power, and we can finally finish the mating!" Lucas kissed her hard, leaving her breathless.

She was just about to pull him back into bed when someone, she thought maybe it was Amelia, yelled, "I left the ceremonial robe outside the door. HURRY THE HELL UP, we don't have all day for you two to get it on again!"

Kaylee reluctantly got dressed, well not really dressed because all she was given was a robe to wear to meet up with her cousins, downstairs. She was a little shocked she had instantly liked the three women; it usually took her a while to warm up to people. They each had qualities Kaylee admired. The easy carefree banter was something Kaylee had always wanted to have with friends, and now, it looked like she might get it with family.

Lucas kissed her and started to leave, and Kaylee wanted to pull him back. She wasn't ready to let him go, even for her cleansing or whatever the fuck it was. He noticed her reluctance and pulled her into a hug.

"I will always be with you, Kaylee, all you need to do is look inside yourself and the bond will connect us. Can you feel it?" he whispered in her ear.

Kaylee closed her eyes and searched her soul, and he was right. She could feel his love and the love she had for him.

"I love you, Lucas, see you soon," she answered with a kiss.

"Count on it, babe," he winked and left.

Tara stood next to her and dramatically swooned, making Amelia catch her. When Amelia pushed her back up, she said, "You are so damn lucky, girl. Lucas is the catch of the century and from the way he was making you scream when we walked up, damn. That's all I can say." Amelia slapped the back of Tara's head to shush her, but that didn't stop Tara. Looking at Kaylee, she fake whisper-yelled, "Amelia is going to get stuck with a mole shifter; he'll need somewhere to go once she starts talking."

Amelia didn't slap her sister this time, but she did give her a dirty look. "Oh, and you, sister dear, are going to mate with a bear shifter. You know the kind who like to spank their women and keep them in line. Big, bad, and dominant. That's what you're going to get."

Tara just shrugged her shoulders and looked at her nails. "That's okay, I like a little slap and tickle. At least my man won't be burrowing into the ground to get away from me. I might even let him tie me up, so he can do all kinds of delicious things to this body," Tara said, rubbing her hands up and down her torso, paying particular attention to her boobs.

Kaylee just laughed. Amelia's face was getting redder by the second. It amazed Kaylee when she meekly replied, "Shut up."

Prue sat down on the couch, noticing her sisters tension and said, "I'm getting a Warlock for a mate. He's going to be sweet and kind, let me continue my work, and help me raise our three children. We're going to live in Maine by the ocean."

Both Amelia and Tara busted up laughing. Kaylee didn't really get what was so funny until Tara said, "Yeah and my ass is purple. You already know who your mate is Prue, and he isn't the sweet, kind, raise the babies while wifey works kind of guy. He's more, Get on my bike bitch and let's ride to where the wind takes us."

Kaylee was stunned and asked, "You know who your mate is, and you're not with him?"

Prue said, "No" at the same time Amelia and Tara said, "Yes."

"I had barely met Lucas and knew I wanted him. How do you do it? How long have you known him?" Kaylee asked, genuinely curious. She loved Lucas and wouldn't change anything about him or their mating. She couldn't imagine denying him, those three weeks had been hell on her.

It wasn't Prue who answered her, but Tara. "She's known him all her life. He's from another Coven and not a respected one. You should see them together, they get all squirmy and uncomfortable; it's hard to watch, but neither of them will budge an inch. Stubborn. Personally, I think Micah is hot—all that leather, those tats, and attitude." Tara said fanning herself. "It's enough to make a girl cream her panties."

Tara and Amelia started arguing, but Kaylee wasn't paying them any attention, she was watching Prue. She looked sad, and it made Kaylee wonder if denying her mate was really the right choice or if Prue was even the one who made the choice in the first place. Poor girl.

"Okay, ladies," Kaylee asked, deciding a change of subject was in order, "tell me what we're supposed to be doing, we're burning daylight here."

Amelia stopped arguing with Tara and said, "We're going to take you to a sacred place all McClane witches have come to on the day of their Ostara. You will be cleansed in the water to prepare yourself for the ceremony. Once the cleansing is complete, Lucas will meet up with us and take you to the ceremonial grounds to present you to the Coven."

"It's really not a big deal," Tara yawned, "you take a bath, we say some things, then the ceremony; blam-o, you're a witch, easy peasy, lemon squeezy."

Kaylee doubted that, but got up and started walking toward the door. "Well then, let's do this thing, ladies. I don't want to keep my man or the Coven waiting."

The walk to the spring wasn't bad, but it was cold out and the robe she was wearing didn't provide her with much coverage. Heck, even the flowy, pastel-colored dresses her cousins were wearing didn't match the weather, and they were all barefoot. Every time Kaylee stepped on a rock or a twig, she let her displeasure be known. The girls just laughed until they started doing the same thing, and Kaylee laughed back at them.

The trip didn't take long, thankfully. She had thought she had been everywhere on her grands property, but Kaylee had never seen this place before. The trail opened up onto a small clearing with a beautiful, small spring in the center, about the size of a twelve-person hot tub. Kaylee looked at it skeptically; it was freaking cold outside; there was no way she was stripping down to get in it, they would have to throw her in.

The three of them joined hands and started to chant. Kaylee was enthralled by the words and melody of the chant. When she looked back at the spring, it had steam coming off of it.

"That was so cool. You three are going to have to teach me how to do that."

"We won't have to. Once the Ostara is complete," Tara laughed, "you'll have this knowledge and much more. Now strip down, sister, and get in. Your body must be cleansed. We've added the herbs of the goddesses to purify your outer being." She winked and whispered, "They make us say that; it's really just some rosemary and lavender, but it smells good." Amelia pushed Tara out of the way and handed Kaylee some soap which looked homemade. Kaylee just looked at it and waited.

"This soap was provided by the High Priestess," Amelia said with flair, even doing a little bow. "It will wipe away the past and help you welcome the future as you clean your body."

"Plus, it smells good, don't forget that," Tara whispered again, making Kaylee laugh.

Prue quietly stepped forward and handed Kaylee a little washcloth. "This was made from the first fabric which touched your body on the day you were born. It is to remember the past, but strive for the future. The day of the Ostara means new beginnings, but we must not forget what we have learned."

Kaylee smiled at Prue and took the cloth made of a very soft, aged cotton. She brought it up to her nose and memories of her past flooded her, things she hadn't remembered before—her father cradling her in his arms, her mother smiling down at her with love shining in her eyes. She took a couple of seconds to let the memories flow over her. The strike of a match and the smell of something burning brought her back to the present.

Kaylee watched as the three women lit sage bundles and started to dance around the spring, chanting. Tara stopped in front of her and said, "Well come on, this part takes a while and you have to be in the water. Don't be shy, we've all seen girl bits and boobies before, no biggie." Tara started to try to help Kaylee take off the robe, practically pushing her into the spring. Kaylee slapped her hands away and did it herself.

Looking at the spring, there was no easy way to do this, so she thought, the hell with it and jumped in. Kaylee came up sputtering, she hadn't expected the water to be so deep. She felt weird skinny dipping by herself while three women she was just starting to get to know, danced around singing, well chanting, waving smoking sticks. But she figured when in Rome and started washing her body and hair. When she was done, her cousins helped her out of the spring and placed the robe back over her shoulders, helping her sit on a rock.

Each one of them brought a different flower to her and placed it in her hair. Amelia was first, holding up her bundle. "This is Celandine, it represents joys to come." Kaylee fingered the tiny yellow flowers before Amelia weaved them into her hair. Tara came forward next with only one flower. "This is a daffodil, it represents new beginnings." Placing it behind Kaylee's ear, she smiled and stepped away.

Prue walked up to her holding a small wreath woven with tiny flowers and ribbon. "This is a wreath made of heather and baby's breath. They represent everlasting love, protection, and wishes which have yet to come true." Prue placed the wreath on Kaylee's head and kissed Kaylee's cheek, making her cry. This was so special.

Kaylee stood and was going to say something, but her emotions were all over the place. Instead, she pulled the three women into her arms and hugged them. "Thank you." Pulling back, she noticed none of them had dry eyes, but they were all smiling, having shared something so special.

Chapter 21

Lucas met Kaylee and her cousins at the trail which led to the sacred grounds. He looked amazing dressed in his ceremonial leathers. He looked every bit the warrior Kaylee knew he was. When he offered her his elbow, Kaylee gladly took it. Coming to the clearing, Kaylee noticed the huge amount of people gathered around in a large circle, but what caught her eye was the woman standing next to her Grandma Ruth. Her mother was here, smiling, but still looking sad. Kaylee smiled back and nodded. This wasn't the time to address the issues they had between them; this moment was more and deserved her whole focus.

"Who presents the Blue Moon Priestess for the Ostara," Grandma Ruth's voice boomed out.

"I do, Lucas Valentin, Alpha of the Valentin Pack and Guardian of the McClane Coven." He smiled at Kaylee, then looked back to Ruth and said, "Mate to Kaylee McClane." Lucas then dropped to his knee with his fist planted against his chest.

Kaylee heard several people gasp at Lucas' statement, but didn't care what any of them thought. They might be family in some way, but she didn't know them. She knew and loved Lucas.

"And do you, Kaylee McClane, accept the Guardian's words?"

"I do." Kaylee placed her hand on Lucas' shoulder. "He is both the Guardian and my mate."

"Well, then, let us begin," Grandma Ruth smiled. With a wave of her hand, a pentagram appeared in a blue blaze from the ground. Kaylee gasped at the sight, but held her ground.

"Kaylee," her mother said, smiling, "the pentagram is a sacred symbol in our culture. The northern point represents the spirit and the other four points represent the elements. By taking your place within, you are accepting its power—spirit, earth, air, fire, and water—all these things contribute to life and the life you choose to lead. Do you willingly take your place?"

Kaylee nodded her head. Grandpa Edwin came forward and guided her to the center of the Pentagram, kissing her hand before releasing her and stepping away. Grandma Ruth began to speak as Kaylee knelt and bowed her head, letting the words flow through her.

"Today is the time of the Spring Equinox. Ostara is a time of equal parts light and dark. Spring has arrived, it is a time of rebirth. The planting season will soon begin, and life will form once more within the earth. As the season welcomes new life and new beginnings, so can we be reborn in the light and love of the gods. Do you, Kaylee, wish to experience the rebirth of Spring and step out of the darkness into the light?"

Kaylee stood, raising her hands to the sky, and said, "Yes, I choose the light." At her words, a bolt of lightning flashed through the sky directly at her. In seconds her mind was reeling with all the knowledge of their Coven—history, spells, people, potions—it was all there. If that wasn't enough, the power she felt hummed underneath her skin. She looked around, but the blue flames had encompassed her, keeping her, blocking her from view. She turned around in a circle seeking out Lucas; she was scared. This was too much, too soon, and she started to panic. Then he was there, walking through the blaze. As he hugged her close, the panic she felt started to calm as did the blaze. Her Grandma Ruth cleared her throat, and Kaylee turned her head to look at her.

"You have been chosen, child, to carry the honor of Blue Moon Priestess. You have also chosen your anchor. Lucas Valentin, do you agree to always be faithful to Kaylee, guard her as you would the pack, and anchor her to the earth, so she may continue on the path of the light?"

Lucas kissed her head and answered, "It is both my honor and my will to do these things for Kaylee, Blue Moon Priestess of the McClane Coven."

"So, has it has been stated, so it will be done. Lucas Valentin, you are released from your guardianship of the McClane Coven and granted the honor as mate, anchor, and warrior to Kaylee. Live, love, and find peace in all you do."

The rest of the Coven chanted the words three times. Lucas kissed Kaylee, showing her without words how much he loved her. Before he could open his eyes to look at her glowing face, someone came up from behind, grabbing Kaylee by the arm.

"Come on, girl, it's time to get your party started."

Kaylee pulled her arm away and looked at him as if he had lost his damn mind. "Who are you and why do you think it's okay to grab me by the arm and try to pull me away?"

Lucas busted out laughing. "Kaylee, this is another one of your cousins, who all seem to be very interrupting today."

"Oh, I'm sorry, I forgot we've never met. Kaylee, I am Brice, your cousin and party planner extraordinaire." He completed his introduction with a curtsy which would put a Disney princess to shame. Kaylee just looked at him for a second, stunned, thinking, is this guy for real? He was gorgeous, but his outfit was outrageous, like Rainbow Bright and My Little Pony threw up all over him in a kaleidoscope of color and glitter, making Kaylee giggle. Kaylee gave him her best curtsy, which was nothing compared to his. Kaylee thought he must have practiced because this shit was hard.

"It's nice to meet you, Brice McClane. Thank you for planning my party."

"Oh, you haven't seen anything yet," he said, giddiness shining in his eyes. "Come now, Kaylee, let's get this party going." With a clap of his hands, he called out, "Girls, let's show Kaylee what we've got!" Tara, Prue, and Amelia joined him on the outskirts of the pentagram, throwing their hands in the air chanting, "May the dark turn to light."

Kaylee was gob smacked when the pentagram, glowing softly a moment ago, changed color, brightened, and started to glow the most beautiful dark blue. It was different, but just as gorgeous, lighting the area like a neon sign.

"Hold on," Brice winked at her, "one more gift for the Blue Moon Priestess." Brice stood in the middle with open arms when a perfect, blue butterfly appeared in the palm of his hand. "The butterfly represents great transformation yet to come. It reminds us our current reality is to be experienced so that we may learn and grow. It is our duty to accept and embrace these changes. Kaylee, you have started by choosing the light, claiming your mate, and accepting your magic into your soul. As your Coven, we celebrate by your side. As your family, we rejoice in the path you have chosen to follow."

Kaylee watched as Brice waved his free hand over the butterfly and it changed into a pendant. She was still staring at his hand when Brice walked to stand in front of her, holding out his hand. "The color blue in a butterfly symbolizes joy, beauty, and luck. Please accept this gift as a reminder of this day and the days yet to come, with joy in your heart, beauty in your soul, and luck by your side."

Kaylee looked to Lucas who was smiling down at her, then she nodded, bending down, allowing Brice to place the necklace around her neck. Brice stepped back, and Kaylee looked up at him, tears in her eyes.

"Welcome, Kaylee Valentin, Blue Moon Priestess of the McClane Coven." Raising his hands above his head, he said, "Let the celebration begin."

Kaylee watched in awe as hundreds of butterflies flew into the air. The sun had set and the moon had risen, providing a glorious backdrop for the colorful butterflies. They flew all around her, rising up into the sky. Fireflies lit the woods in the most beautiful way as if it was glittering. Holding her hands out, she spun in a circle, taking everything in. Kaylee stopped and threw herself into Lucas' arms, never doubting he would catch her.

"It's all so beautiful. Lucas, did you see, can you feel it?"

"The most beautiful thing I see is right here in my arms. I love you, Kaylee. Congratulations, baby."

"This day has turned out so perfectly, I'm so blessed to have you here with me at my side."

Lucas leaned down, kissing her deeply. It was as if everything around them disappeared and only the two of them remained. Kaylee accepted the gift he was giving her, letting all her past worries leave her body and accepted the future was in her hands. The moment was lost when Brice grabbed one of Lucas' arms, loosening his hold on her. Lucas growled, but Kaylee just laughed.

"Lucas, bring your mate to the middle and share a dance with her," Brice said as music, from out of nowhere, started to fill the woods. They made their way to the center of the pentagram which was no longer there. The grass had covered it back over and only the blue star could be seen.

Lucas bowed in front of her. "May I have this dance, Kaylee Valentin?" Kaylee giggled and returned the favor, curtsying, holding out her hand. "Yes, you may, kind sir, please lead the way."

As they begin to dance, Kaylee looked around. Tara and Brice were dancing together in a way which could only be described as lewd, but comical. Her grands were off to one side, holding each other close. Prue and Amelia were laughing, doing a weird version of a waltz together. All around her, people were happily celebrating.

She noticed her mother looking at her with a huge grin on her face, a few tears in her eyes. She acknowledged Kaylee with a nod, then blew her a kiss. It would take a long time for the two of them to recover from all Kaylee had learned, but knowing that her mother came here to support her meant the world to her. Someday, they would get there, she just hoped it was soon.

Tara and Brice danced closer to them, shaking their butts and laughing. Lucas and Kaylee watched and laughed right alongside them. Lucas had even stopped the slow sway they had been doing and added a few moves to compete with Brice. When Brice came up behind Lucas and started to dance, Kaylee laughed, pulling Lucas away, waving her finger at Brice. He shrugged his shoulders and kept dancing.

When all the hairs on the back of her neck lifted, Kaylee stopped, and holding on to Lucas, whispered, "I sense something isn't right."

"Oh Kaylee," Lucas said, "he's just a little feminine and maybe he likes men, but he can hold his own with the best of us when it comes to fighting."

"What the hell are you talking about Lucas?" Kaylee had the most serious look on her face. "Stop listening to the music and looking at the lights. I'm not talking about Brice! Something isn't right in these woods tonight; use your senses, Luc."

Lucas closed his eyes, blocking everything else out. Kaylee was right, there was something or rather someone out of place. He smelled the blood of his maker, but this was different, mixed and more potent, somehow, another hybrid.

"Stay here, Kaylee, Atticus is in the woods." Kaylee grabbed his arm, not wanting him to go, but Lucas pulled away. "Trust me, Kaylee, I need to find out what he's up to. Brice, take her, please," Lucas barked out.

Kaylee watched as her previously flamboyant cousin turned into a very serious Warlock. "Come, Kaylee, let your warrior do his job."

"He can't go out there alone, Brice," Kaylee protested. "Something could happen to him, I have to go with him." Kaylee started to struggle, but Brice's grip was strong.

"Kaylee, this his duty; he's strong, his pack is standing guard, and we have twenty witches who will step in at a moment's notice if needed. You need to trust in your man and his abilities. He can't do what needs to be done if he's worried about you. Your powers are new, untested; you would only be a distraction."

Chastised, Kaylee watched, helplessly, as Lucas walked out of the circle and into the woods, vowing to herself that one day she would be strong enough to stand by his side.

Chapter 22

Atticus watched the ceremony from the wooded shadows. He was too late. Well, not really, he had been there, but chose not to stop it or even attempt to take Kaylee Smith, now Valentin.

The ceremony was over, and Kaylee had chosen the path of the light. He didn't really care, but Bane would be furious, and he knew his Master would make him pay. Pissing Bane off had become one of Atticus's favorite past times. Just thinking about his Master made Atticus' stomach churn.

He remembered the days before he was turned and all the promises Bane had made, all of them lies except for one; he did have great power. But that power had been hard earned, not taught. Atticus had spent years gaining knowledge and power, trying his best to figure out a way to be released from the vile man.

Watching Lucas, he was a little jealous. Lucas had resisted Bane's charms—something Atticus couldn't say for himself—gaining a life Atticus craved. When Bane had lured him from the safety of his pack, Atticus didn't think he had a choice and accepted the monster's terms. Now he knew better, Lucas had proven that to him. It was one of the reasons he was giving his brother this gift.

Atticus could smell the pack surrounding him and let them come. He could have left, but this was one confrontation which needed to happen. There were things he needed to tell Lucas and another matter Atticus needed to attend to, the most important matter; he could sense her nearby, his mate.

Atticus wasn't the least bit concerned when Lucas stepped in front of him, only slightly straightening himself from his position leaning against the tree. He grinned at the arrogance Lucas showed. This man didn't consider him an equal, but would soon learn to never underestimate an opponent.

"Who are you? Why are you here?"

"Please, let's stop these stupid games. You know exactly who I am. The witches are watching, and I know for a fact, the old hag has already filled you in."

"You will have respect for these lands and the ones who rule it," Lucas boomed. "That hag is the High Priestess of the McClane Coven. As a Were, you would do well to watch your tongue unless you would rather have it removed from your mouth, Atticus."

"Ah, I see you've heard of me. That's good to know, but I see my name hasn't brought the fear I'd hoped. Tell me Lucas, Alpha of the Valentin pack, mate to the Blue Moon Priestess, and former Guardian of the McClane Coven, do you believe your mate is safe? Do you believe he will just let her power go now the ceremony is complete?"

"I believe, brother," Lucas grabbed Atticus until they were nose to nose, "I can protect what is mine from anything you or Bane has planned. I believe with the McClane witches at my side and my pack at my back, neither of you will stand a chance at harming Kaylee."

Atticus pushed Lucas away, showing him a small portion of his strength. They were well matched, but Atticus had the advantage of the dark magic coursing through his body.

"Then you're a fool. Bane is in her mind, in her blood. Her Coven and family have let your mate down. He has been there all her life, and he will have her."

Lucas charged him, taking Atticus to the ground. Atticus allowed it, just this once; it wouldn't happen again.

"What are you talking about? Bane has never come near Kaylee," Lucas yelled.

Atticus rolled away after landing a few blows of his own. "Ask her mother, she knows. James Smith made a deal with the devil, and Kaylee is the one who will pay the price."

Atticus watched as Lucas started to strip out of his clothes, preparing to shift. He wasn't opposed, he wanted to see how well matched their animals would be, but there wasn't time. Holding up his hand, he said, "Stop I'm not here to fight you. If that was the case, I wouldn't have allowed the ceremony to proceed. I'm here only to warn you and make you aware of what is yet to come."

"And why is that, Atticus? Aren't you Bane's little puppet, his enforcer, the one he sends to carry out all his dirty little deeds? Tell me does that include luring the young men he likes so much to his bed?"

Those words infuriated Atticus and brought up way too many memories. Atticus retaliated, grabbing Lucas, punching him several times.

"I see we both know what our Master demands," Atticus said between gritted teeth.

"I don't have a Master, Atticus. That's a disgrace only you hold," Lucas growled.

"Not for long. Remember my words, brother. Bane is coming for you and your mate. He will have you both under his command and in his bed before long unless you pay attention and take this threat seriously. I will not interfere again."

"Why? Because like a good little puppet you're going to run back to your Master with your tail between your legs?"

"No, because I'm taking what is mine."

"And what exactly do you think is yours?"

Atticus moved quickly, knocking the werewolf standing next to his mate on his ass. Wrapping his arms around her body, he looked at Lucas. "You have your salvation, now I'll take mine." Danica screamed, and the two of them were gone.

Lucas looked around; the remainder of his pack was standing, staring at the same place he was. "Find them!" Eric, Dylan, and Macon shifted, taking off through the woods, but Lucas knew they wouldn't find anything. Atticus had flashed, something Lucas had heard about, but never witnessed.

His scent was still in the air, along with Danica's, but it was stationary. There would be no trail. Going to Matt, he helped him up. Matt tried to pull away, but Lucas didn't let him.

"Let go, Luc, I have to find her!"

"No, you have to stay here and help me protect Kaylee. Didn't you hear what Atticus said?"

"I heard him, damn it, but I have to get her back."

"Stop it, use your senses, they aren't here, you'll never find them. We have to do what needs to be done, now. Build our bond, become what has always been meant to be, twin Alpha's, born and bred. It's the only way we can keep Kaylee safe."

"And, what, just forget about Dani? No, I don't accept that. I failed her once, I will not do it again. I can't believe you would even ask me to."

"I love Dani as much as you do, Matt, but you heard him, he won't hurt her. He thinks she's his mate, his salvation. We'll find a way to bring

138

her back, but we need to stick together, work together. Can't you see that?"

Lucas felt her before he saw her; Kaylee stood by his side, reaching for his hand. "Let him go, Lucas, it's what is meant to be. This is his journey, you can't keep him here because of me."

"Kaylee!"

"No." Looking at Matt, she said, "Find her, Matt, and bring her home, but watch closely, things are never as they first seem. Keep your mind open and your senses sharp. Atticus isn't the enemy, he's one of us. He just hasn't found his place yet, much like you."

The End – For now...

Atticus & Danica's story –
Dirt Road Redemption Coming Spring 2018

Authors Note:

Livell James – A little about me. I am lover of all things inspiring and a multitude of art forms. I have told stories with photography for many years and decided to put pen to paper for the stories I feel can only be told with my words. My debut story in a planned series is paranormal romance co-written by fellow Author Chelsea Handcock. When I am not writing or taking photos, I enjoy spending time with my wife and checking items off my bucket list.

Chelsea Handcock – I am honored to have had the pleasure of writing this story along with a good friend, Livell James. I have been an admirer of his photography for quite some time. When he shared his ideas with me for this book I became inspired. I hope our combined words, will provide the same for everyone that reads it.

Now we both would like to thanks for very special people. Tammie Smith and Cody Criswell, two truly extraordinary people, your photos brought this story to life for Livell and drew me in. Tammie, a woman of many talents also worked tirelessly with Livell to make the book cover perfect, we can't thank you enough. Sandy Ebel with Personal Touch Editing, you kept your promise and made our words shine. DeAnne, thank you so much for being our beta reader, your thoughts and suggestions have enhanced the book to new levels. We would also like to thank both our spouses and families for always being supportive, constantly challenging us and encouraging us along the way.

To our readers, thanks for giving this series a chance. We hope you stick with us and discover all the trials and tribulations yet to come. We hope we have left you guessing, but most of all, we hope I leave you intrigued. Enjoy the ride and happy reading.
Please check out www.chelseahandcock.com for updates and future books. You can also reach either of us on Facebook at any time, https://www.facebook.com/livell.james.5, https://www.facebook.com/AuthorChelseaHandcock/.